I would like to dedicate the book to anyone who has suffered abuse, whether it was verbal, mental, emotional or physical

THE FIND

The air had taken on an autumn chill. The first flash flood in living memory had now subsided. The raging torrent of water of the previous day had swept down from the hills, collapsing a dry-stone wall in its path, allowing the water to flood the lower land.

All that was left was the debris scattered at the height of the water's edge. Branches, leaves and fencing posts littered the small fields, giving away the tell-tale signs of what had taken place. The long grass had been flattened on the banks of the stream by the weight of the raging water.

Nigel Brown, the farmhand, observed the scene as he strode out towards the wood. He was a lanky lad, wearing an old pair of jeans ripped on one knee. His old brown jumper covered his thin frame. His straggly mousy brown hair flew back in the breeze.

The mud beneath him squelched and splashed his Wellington boots. He carried an old iron bowl containing grain for the hens. He could see in the wood the sun's rays filtering through the branches and leaves, like shafts of light.

He noticed a white object on the ground tucked away in the debris, illuminated by the streaming light. As he walked closer, he couldn't decide what it was. Perhaps a stone washed down in the flood.

Horror struck when he realised its significance. He turned it over with his boot for confirmation and he knew then for certain, it was a human skull! The eye sockets seemed to stare back at him with cold darkness.

He immediately dropped the bowl, spilling some grain, and turned and ran back up to the farm buildings, shouting for the farmer. Neil Dale appeared from around the cooling house. He was wearing blue overalls; he sauntered towards Nigel.

"What's up wi you, lad, you look as if you've sen a ghost."

"There's a human skull in the wood," Nigel shouted, trying to get his breath back.

"Don't talk rubbish, lad, it's probably an animal's skull."

"Come and see for yourself, if you don't believe me," Nigel retorted.

They both set off to the wood in silence. The sun had disappeared behind a cloud, so the skull was no longer visible in the sun's rays.

"It was here, I saw it, I know it's here somewhere." Nigel continued to search where he thought he had seen it, kicking up the dirt and debris with his dirty wellington boot. "Here it is, I told you I'd seen it."

Neil bent over his tall, sturdy frame to inspect it. "Looks as if she's been dead centuries."

"How do you know it's a she?" Nigel demanded to know.

"I just thought it was a smaller skull than a man's skull, that's all," Neil said convincingly.

Nigel responded, "It could be a boy."

"You're probably right, lad, it's a boy, died ages ago. Now don't be telling anyone, I don't want the whole farm dug up looking for more ancient bones." Neil instructed the farmhand to bury it and forget about the whole thing.

Nigel picked up the bowl he had left and opened the sliding door, to let the hens out of the small shed. He scattered the remaining grain left in the bowl, on some dry ground. He returned to the buildings to find a suitable spade to bury the skull.

Lying in bed that night, Nigel could not get the sight of the skull out of his head. Those eye sockets staring up at him had deeply disturbed him.

He tossed and turned in bed, the farmer's words going around and around in his aching head. He thought he should tell someone but was frightened of losing his job.

He was only 17 years old and work was hard to come by. Most farmers had sons or staff to help on their farms and didn't want inexperienced workers like him.

Neil had some staff, but it was a large intensive farm, so it needed more hands. Nigel had always wanted to farm; he loved the outdoor life and the animals.

His parents were not farmers – they worked at the local dairy in Townsfoot about five miles east of the village of Finley, where he lived.

Several weeks of disturbed nights were taking their toll.

"Wake up, wake up. What are you doing falling asleep over your supper? Is he working you too hard?" It was his mother waking him violently with a shake.

He was stunned for a few seconds then turned to his mother and asked, "If I told you something will you keep it a secret?"

"Well, that depends," she replied with her arms akimbo.

"What I have to say must go no further than these four walls, promise me," Nigel whispered.

"I promise," she said meekly.

Nigel explained the whole story. His mother listened intently, her eyes widening as the story unfolded. Then silence.

"Well say something!" Nigel said in a raised voice.

His mother looked shocked. "I think you should tell the police, son." Her voice was soft and quiet.

"No, no I can't tell the police, I'll lose my job!" he protested loudly.

"I'll tell you something, my boy, that farmer Neil, he was married to a young woman, Emily. She was supposed to have run off with a travelling salesman. No one has seen her since, not even her parents!"

Nigel slumped back in his chair shocked at what he had just heard.

"Mind you, I heard she was never happy at home or with him, poor soul. You must tell the police, or I will," she shouted.

"You promised, Mum, you promised," screamed Nigel, angry about the whole thing. Nigel stomped out of the room and went for a walk to calm himself down. His mother heard the front door of the cottage slam shut behind him.

She thought hard through the night, about what had been said. The guilt tore at her core for not phoning the police immediately.

The next day, she decided to ring Townsfoot Police Station and told them exactly what her son had told her. She recorded it in her diary, 1st November 1982.

The police arrived on the doorstep very quickly, wanting to interview Nigel. It was his day off. They found Nigel on the village green talking to some friends. He was led away and driven back to his cottage at the far end of the village, in a police car.

He felt betrayed and very embarrassed in front of his friends. Nigel was really afraid; his mother could have 'opened up a can of worms' and he could lose his job.

The two policemen were very patient and kind during the interview. Nigel was so nervous, he was a quiet, shy lad. His right leg was shaking, moving up and down with nerves, and he was anxiously biting the side of his left thumb.

He told them what he knew. The police asked him to accompany them to the farm and show them where he had buried the skull.

They left but it wasn't long before several police cars and a van were seen driving through the village, heading towards the farm. Neil Dale, the farmer and owner of the land, was very cooperative and allowed them into the wood.

It took a while for Nigel to find the skull again. He had hidden it very well and covered it over with leaves to match the rest of the surrounding area.

The area was cordoned off. There was about a fifty acre stretch to search for the rest of the skeleton that may have been washed further down during the flash flood, into the large swollen river below.

Neil Dale was being questioned in the farmhouse. He was calm and composed and he was as surprised as everyone else at finding a skull on his land.

The police found a leg bone further down in the wood and were confident about finding more of the skeleton. The light was fading so the search had to resume the following day.

Nigel walked through the fields on the well-trodden public footpath. It was 5.30 am, it was still dark; his torch light lit the mile walk from his cottage, into the farm yard. He had been thinking a lot about the events of the previous day.

He didn't know if he still had a job, Neil was sure to blame him. Neil was there rinsing his hands off in a water trough.

"I didn't think I'd see you, lad, again," Neil said, looking up at Nigel. He was thinking Nigel would suspect he was a killer and stay away.

"I want to come back to work if you will have me. It was Mum that told the police not me. She promised me she wouldn't tell. I know you didn't do what folks are saying about you," Nigel nervously blurted out.

"And what would that be, lad?" Neil questioned, wiping his wet hands down his dirty overalls to dry them.

"They're saying you murdered Emily," he replied sheepishly.

Neil laughed. "Ah rubbish, now you get back to work and don't listen to gossip."

It was a wet, miserable day for the team of police to resume searching every inch of ground. They combed the area in a line across the designated area with sticks, but nothing more was found.

The leg bone had been identified as being from a young male adult. The skull was from a young female adult. This surprised everyone as they assumed at first it was from one skeleton. Now there could be a serial killer at large as the bones were not centuries old as Neil had assumed.

Later that morning, Neil had been asked to go to the Police Station to help with furthering their enquiries. He agreed without hesitation.

He did protest his innocence and said it could have been anyone dumping and burying bodies on his land as the wood was quite close to the road. The police were now treating him as their main suspect.

The police detectives were very interested in hearing about his marriage to Emily and where she had gone. Neil didn't know.

He repeatedly told them she was making eyes at a travelling salesman called Ken, and he assumed that they had run off together when she didn't return from a shopping trip to Townsfoot.

She had gone on the bus as Neil was changing the oil on her car. He couldn't remember the date but it was sometime in November 1971, eleven years ago. He was building a cowshed that year which helped his memory.

"The ungrateful cow," he told them. "I gave her everything she had."

The police wanted to know what she had taken with her and listed things to jog his memory – clothes, cheque book, money, jewellery, family photographs.

Neil could only say she took her handbag, the usual cash for shopping and her shopping bags. He described roughly what she would have worn.

"Where are her other belongings now?" they asked. Neil had given her belongings back to her parents as he didn't want to be reminded of her – he was very angry with her for leaving him.

They quizzed him about her life insurance. "Who was the beneficiary if she died and how much was the policy worth on her death?" they asked.

Neil confessed he didn't like paying for insurance apart from what he had to pay on the house and the farm buildings and the farm stock. Neither of them had life insurance.

He was questioned further about the travelling salesman. They wanted his full name, a description of him, who he worked for. What make and colour of a car he drove and the registration number.

Neil remembered he was called Ken but couldn't remember much more, other than he was smart and clean shaven. He sold household products like dish clothes, tea towels and clothes lines. He drove a green Morris Mini van.

The interview continued and lasted over five hours. He was questioned over and over again to see if his story changed, but Neil remained consistent.

The day before, the crime scene had been photographed, the items bagged and tagged and taken away for more detailed forensic analysis. Neil's two rifles were also taken away.

There was nothing more to do, no more items had been found that day. The flood water had unfortunately destroyed most of the crime scene.

A search warrant had been served to search Neil's Farm and the house but nothing was found of interest to add to the case.

Neil's partner Janet Bennett had looked on in dismay and was disgusted as the detectives rummaged through every drawer, cupboard and wardrobe, even the attic. She was briefly questioned but had little to say.

After Neil's interview he was driven home at 3pm, giving him enough time to feed the heifers and beef cattle. He was tired and looked drained.

He arrived at the back door of his house, for tea, and went into the vestibule. He removed his overalls, rolling them down around his wellington boots and then slipped his feet out of them.

In the large farmhouse kitchen, Janet was looking upset – she wasn't coping very well with all the disruption and intrusion of the police.

They hugged each other and Neil lightly kissed her on her forehead.

"Chin up, lass, it will be all over soon and we can get back to normal." He then told her all about his interview with the police.

Janet placed a blue beaker of milk on the table for four-year-old Luke and turned, saying, "My life has been turned upside down. I can't believe this is happening to us."

They sat down at the long wooden table. Neil ruffled Luke's dark brown hair and smiled at his young son. The grandfather clock in the hallway struck 4 o'clock.

Neil picked up his pint mug of tea and filled his plate with cheese sandwiches and homemade cherry cake.

Jenny, aged two years, toddled into the kitchen, with her pink toy rabbit and showed it to her Daddy. Neil sat her on his lap and played with her shiny jet-black curls of hair.

Janet continued to moan. "They went through everything, even my knicker drawer!" she explained. "There is no privacy, we haven't done anything wrong, so why should we have to suffer?"

"Hush now, don't upset the kids," Neil said calmingly. "I'll be late milking tonight; we didn't get everything done this afternoon with all the carry on."

"Oh, by the way, there was a strange phone call this afternoon besides the press. He wanted to speak to you," Janet remembered. "I said you were not available. He refused to give his name, he said he would ring again. He said something like, we would be crawling with police here."

"Perhaps it was just the press," Neil muttered.

Janet added, "I see it's all been on the national news and cars have been stopping and parking up on the top road all day. People getting out with their binoculars, trying to see what's going on here."

She sipped her tea and watched Luke playing with his toy tractor on the table; he was oblivious to the seriousness of the day's events.

"Well, that's me done," Neil said, rubbing his belly. "Now don't worry, I'll see you about seven and later I'll call in at the pub after supper."

He returned to the vestibule dipping his right toe into his wellington boot and then the other. He unrolled his overalls up over his body and slid his arms into the sleeves and left.

Janet could hear him striding out across the yard. The lights dimmed momentarily in the kitchen as he pressed the button in the cooling house, to start off the milking process. A constant hum could be heard.

Nigel had already got everything ready for milking and was starting to get the buckets ready for feeding the calves.

The local pub, The Bull, was packed out that night. Locals desperate to hear about the news. The pub was thick with cigarette smoke and the smell of beer.

The loud hum of voices saturated the air. It was a quaint little public house, small rooms and low ceilings. The taller men had to duck under the oak beams, adorned with horse brasses.

The open fire had a small log fire burning and smouldering away, sparks occasionally flying up the blackened chimney. The smell of the burning wood mingled with the aroma of beer, cigarettes and pipe tobacco smoke.

"I bet Neil murdered them both, they wouldn't get a chance to run away," said one gruff voice.

"He has his rages, that's for sure," said another.

"I hope they get him, Emily was a sweet lass, he didn't deserve her," another voice added.

The heavy latched door suddenly opened and everyone went silent. There in the doorway was the six-foot, well-built frame of Neil Dale. His messy black hair partly covered his unshaven face. He glared at everyone. He strode confidently towards the old wooden bar and ordered a beer from the elderly barman.

Everyone turned away and spoke quietly to each other, changing the subject that had excited them earlier. Many people were afraid of Neil. He had had plenty of battles with his neighbours over the years.

Neil supped his beer at the bar. A few called out acknowledging his presence. He just grunted back in reply. He didn't want conversation. He soon left; he was just putting in an appearance to show everyone he was carrying on as normal.

When Nigel Brown got home the following night, the local newspaper, The Finley Post, was laid out on the kitchen table. The front-page headline 'Double murder' screamed out at him.

He picked it up and began reading the article. His mother came into the room with a basket full of laundry.

"I don't think they know any more than we do," she said, disappointed.

"Well it wasn't Neil. He was OK with me yesterday and today. I thought he was going to give me the sack for telling–"

"You didn't tell him it was me who rung the police, did you?" she screamed.

Nigel ran up to his room out of the way. He was fed up of all the gossip that had stirred up this sleepy village. He just wanted to forget about it and get back to a normal life.

Nigel came downstairs later to watch the television, eating his supper from a tray on his lap. During the break he went to make himself another mug of tea in the kitchen. His mother was busy making an apple pie.

The Rayburn was radiating a lovely warm feel to the room and the smell of jam tarts in the oven was also inviting.

"Was the skull intact?" his mother asked curiously.

"Oh, Mum, forget about it," Nigel moaned as he filled the kettle with water from the old fashion tap.

"Just asking," she said, putting the pie in the oven.

"If you must know, the skull was smashed at the base and it had no lower jaw, and only one back tooth... I can't believe he did it... he wouldn't do such a thing."

That night Nigel lay in his bed staring at the vaulted ceiling in his room. He was happy he hadn't lost his job but very unsettled about the search at the farm he had witnessed.

A little doubt had entered his mind; perhaps Neil had killed them both – what would happen to the farm if Neil was sent to prison, he thought.

The police search had been very thorough, even tractor boxes had been searched. He wondered what they were looking for. They had spent a lot of time in Neil's office going through all his papers, bank statements and the farm's files.

They searched the farm's workshop where they kept all the small tools, ropes, welding machine, grinder, vices and generator. There were other machines like the chain saw and a circular saw.

Most of it was fairly new, as Neil had got rid of his father's old tools and machinery last year, at the auction in Townsfoot.

His car and Land Rover were searched as well. They didn't find anything. It had been eleven years since Emily had disappeared, so it was unlikely, they would find anything as they were different vehicles anyway, he mused.

There was a pit where Neil burnt rubbish – that was even searched. He wondered whether they were looking for more bodies; perhaps they thought Neil was a serial killer and had killed more people! All the events of the day whirled around his head until finally he fell asleep with exhaustion.

Nigel's mother visited the village post office and store the following day, carrying her shopping basket.

"Hello," called a voice from behind the store counter. "Can I help you get anything?"

Nigel's mother placed a box of matches and a bottle of washing up liquid on the counter.

"Well, I think the police have just about finished their house-to-house enquiries," the shopkeeper informed her.

She continued chatting. "They were asking me the date when Emily disappeared. Strange as it was on my birthday, 26th November. I couldn't remember the year, but the police said it was 1971."

"That was lucky for them, you having a birthday on that date – how did you remember Emily disappeared then? I hadn't a clue," replied Nigel's mother.

"Our Jean was on the bus when Emily was on, so she was expecting her to return on the only bus back at 4 o'clock from Townsfoot. She wondered where she was and what Neil would do if she was late back."

"Poor girl, I hope it wasn't her in the wood; she was such a lovely girl. Perhaps she did run off with that salesman after all, Neil did say she had at the time," pondered Nigel's mother.

"The police will probably be trying to track down the travelling salesman, if he exists, that is. I never saw him – did you?" queried the shopkeeper.

"Well, I've had salesmen knocking at our door but I couldn't say if it was him – 11 years ago is a long time to remember," came the reply. Nigel's mother eventually left and returned home.

The police paid a visit to Emily's parents, Brian and Margaret Hunt, at their farm, Browtop Farm in Brow. It was about 10 miles from Finley.

The policeman wanted to know where their daughter now lived to eliminate her from their enquiries.

They didn't know. Neil had told them she had run off with a travelling salesman called Ken. They believed him, they considered Neil the son they never had and were very fond of him.

The policeman asked them why Emily would want to run away, was the marriage in difficulty or was she just unhappy with her life?

The parents were as surprised as everyone else that she had run off. Neil had given her a good life; she lived in a big house and had her own car; she wanted for nothing.

The policeman wanted to know if they had any of Emily's belongings and if she kept a diary. They told him they had been given her belongings just before Janet moved in to the farmhouse in about 1977. Neil had told them; he had sold Emily's jewellery that he had given her.

Margaret, her mother, had given Emily's belongings away to the charity shop in Townsfoot. Her clothes were far too small for Margaret to wear.

Emily was never interested in writing so it was unlikely she ever kept a diary. Animals and nature were her passions in life, the policeman was told.

The policeman thought it was odd to choose a life with a travelling salesman and leave the animals and the farm.

The case was beginning to stall. The police thought Neil was involved but couldn't link him to the skull or the leg bone at this stage, apart from that they were found on his land.

He didn't appear to have a concrete motive either. The police returned his rifles – there was no evidence they were used in any crime.

The police were finding it difficult, with the sparse information received, to find Ken, the travelling salesman. They needed to eliminate him from their enquiries.

IT'S TOO SHALLOW

Emily was born in January 1951, the only child of poor tenant farmers. Her father, Brian Hunt, was average height with curly red hair.

Margaret, her mother, was small and chubby with straight long black hair tied back. She always wore a flowered pinafore apron over her dress, blouse and cardigan.

They farmed a 120-acre hill farm and had mainly Swaledale sheep, a small beef herd and a few hens. There was about 30 acres of meadows and the rest rough grazing land.

Brian had a part-time job at the slaughter house for parts of the year, in the nearest town of Canley. Margaret worked at home and on the farm.

They had tried for a while to conceive Emily. So, when she was born, they were delighted. Although they had hoped for a boy, they were doting parents for her baby years.

She was a lovely baby; she would feed contentedly. When her nappy was changed, she would lie in her handmade cot and quickly fall asleep. Later she showed a lot of humour and loved to giggle and laugh. She was such a joy to them.

One of Emily's early memories was the river. They often spent their free time as an extended family at the river, where there was a quiet little pool, ideal for a three-year-old to learn to swim.

"Come to me, Emily," coaxed her father as he held out his arms to encourage her into the warm water.

"It's too shallow, Daddy," Emily shouted.

They all laughed at her mixing up her words. She stepped forward into her father's arms. She felt safe and secure, and splashed the water with her legs excitedly, laughing and giggling.

The small tenanted farm house was very basic. There was an outside toilet down the garden path and across a small yard.

It was too high for Emily to sit on the wooden seat, so she had an old chamber pot under her bed and a small bucket downstairs behind the kitchen door to use.

The kitchen had an old range built partly into an alcove in the wall. A drying rack hung from the ceiling, washing was always drying or airing there from the heat of the range.

They still had the old glazed stone sink, with the blue rimmed enamel bowl to wash up in. The cupboards and sets of drawers were free standing.

There was a walk-in pantry leading off from the kitchen. Wooden shelves lined the walls. Stone slabs supported on walls, kept the food cool. There was no window, just a vent covered by mesh made of metal.

The old tin bath hung on the wall in the wash house. Emily had her baths in front of the range to keep her warm. Her pyjamas would be warming on the rail ready for her to dress for bed.

Her long hair was washed with soap; vinegar was used in the last rinse. This made her beautiful dark chestnut hair shine.

On warm sunny days she would run up the hill and let the warm breeze run through her hair, to dry it. One day Nipper, the Jack Russell, joined her.

At the top of the hill she felt ill and dizzy so she lay down in the short grass. Nipper faithfully stayed by her, cuddling up to her, so she could stay warm.

"Where is Emily?" Brian asked, returning for his supper, from the outside.

"She went for a run up the hill to dry her hair, but that was a while ago. See if you can see her," his wife replied.

Brian found her and picked her up in his arms; she looked very pale. Not the usual ruddy cheeks. He kissed her gently on the forehead and carried her home in his strong arms.

Emily was suffering from flu and was very ill for several weeks. She was confined to bed and kept warm with a large quilt covering her.

Lying in bed, she could see the rolling hills through her little bedroom window. The sheep dotted the hilly landscape. She would watch the many shapes of clouds floating by, trying to make pictures out of them.

Her room was sparse; a small rug covered the dark wooden floorboards near her bed. She had a heavy walnut wardrobe with a drawer underneath and a small open fireplace.

Her small brush and comb were placed neatly on the wooden windowsill. She had a rag doll her mother had made and a teddy bear sat beside her in bed.

As she was growing up, she grew to love the farm cats and their little kittens. She had names for all of them. She usually fed them every morning, with milk and leftovers from the kitchen.

They were kept hungry so they would catch the mice. The mother cats would call out as they brought home young rabbits, to feed their kittens as well as the mice. It was a big scramble to feed first from the carcass.

Birds' feathers were often seen around the yard, a telling sign the birds didn't fly away quickly enough from the cat's claws, another meal for the kittens.

Emily also saw tiny featherless birds that had fallen from their nests. She would pick them up with a bucket and spade, and bury them in the garden. She would always say a little prayer for them.

She loved all creatures. She was fascinated with ladybirds – how they opened their black spotted red case releasing the delicate wings underneath, to fly away.

Without siblings she had plenty of time to observe the wonderful nature evolving around her. Watching caterpillars chomping through vegetation, bloating up with food. Spinning a cocoon and evolving as a beautiful butterfly.

She would chase the white cabbage butterfly off her mother's cabbages in the vegetable garden. Delighted with how they darted away from her, she never caught any.

She would watch for an hour for a spider to complete its web, fascinated by its skilled work. She often popped back to see if it had caught a fly and to see the spider wrap it round in silk thread.

The working sheep dog, Shep, was usually chained up to his kennel out in the yard when he was not working. She saw he hadn't any bedding. So, she gathered some straw up from the yard barn floor and took it into his kennel.

Shep kindly let her in but wouldn't let her out. He grabbed hold of her right arm and locked his jaw. She screamed in pain and fright.

Both her parents came running from different directions at the sound of the piercing screams. The dog released her. She ran towards them, blood streaming down her arm.

She cried uncontrollably. Her mother wrapped her arm in a clean tea towel and drove her to the doctor's house in Canley.

It was a large house stood in about an acre of beautiful gardens. Dr Shaw had a waiting room and a surgery downstairs.

The doctor washed the swollen and bruised wound. It was ugly and needed stitches. Emily would remember the event very clearly all her life and carried the scars of this traumatic experience.

While they were away, Brian shot the dog using his rifle.

"That'll teach you, you mad dog," he said angrily.

He buried it before they arrived back. Emily cried that night; she blamed herself for Shep being killed. She knew he was defending his home and she should not have gone in.

Later, her father got another Border Collie sheep dog, called Ben. Emily was very afraid of him at first but then they became good friends.

They would both enjoy running together. She would throw sticks for him – he would not always give them back, but he was a kind natured dog.

Emily's parents started to argue as she turned four. She didn't know why. She could hear them in the evening shouting at each other as she lay in bed. Her happy young life had appeared to have ended.

Her mother started to shout at her too. She had to do more jobs. She would get up with her parents at 6.30 am.

She was expected to feed the cats, dogs and the hens with food already prepared for her.

She would giggle at the way the cats came running from all directions, tails straight up, when she shouted "Cush, Cush," at the top of her voice. She would watch the dogs wolf down their food.

She enjoyed walking into the corner of the meadow to let the hens out of their coop and to scatter the grain on the ground. She would pause to watch them all clucking and pecking.

Every morning, Emily would set the table for breakfast. She had a bowl of porridge made by her mother, in a large iron pan on the range. Her parents had rashers of bacon with fried eggs, as well.

She had morning chores to do, helping her mother sort the washing. Washing was done the old-fashioned way, in a big cast iron tub with a fire lit beneath it, in the outside wash house.

The deep metal tub was placed in a large stone slab with a round hole in it. The supporting walls were made of stone. Nothing had been modernised on this tenanted farm.

Water was piped from a spring that flowed out of the hillside. It never ran dry. During heavy rain it was a bit cloudy. The water for human consumption was always boiled on the range. Waste was piped and collected in an underground sewage tank in the meadow.

Emily wasn't strong enough yet to turn the mangle's handle, to squeeze the water out of the washing but she watched her mother wring out the clothes.

She helped pass the clothes to her mother to peg out on the line in the garden. She would watch the wind fill the sleeves and trouser legs and see the towels flap like birds' wings. Emily could see fun in everything.

Sheets were folded a certain way – her mother was very particular – and towels too. She helped her mother bake and watched her lay the fires in the grates.

One night her mother was in a particularly bad mood. She burst into her bedroom.

"Don't be using your pot tonight. I don't want the bother of emptying it in the morning," she told her abruptly.

Emily tried not to think about having to go but she was desperate. Finally, she couldn't wait or she would wet the bed, then her mother would be very cross indeed.

She used her chamber pot and poured her urine through a crack in the floorboards! They must have known as the ceiling became stained downstairs. Fortunately, no one said anything.

Her mother ordered her to come into the sitting room one evening. The fire was blazing in the grate, Nipper was lying in his usual place on the rug in front of the fire.

A bowl of hot water was in her mother's hand.

"Hold this," she said, sitting herself in the armchair. Emily complied.

Her mother dipped a cloth into the hot water and squeezed out the excess. Then applied it to the boil on her knee.

Emily found the bowl too hot after a while and dropped it; it was burning her fingers.

"Stupid girl," her mother shouted as she slapped Emily across the face. Emily ran crying to her room. Nipper darted after her.

Emily and Nipper curled up on her bed and cuddled each other. She couldn't understand adults and why they were so mean to her. She only understood her animals.

When Emily started school, it was a big shock to her. She rarely saw other children, only her older cousins at holiday times.

Emily was shy and quiet but soon made friends. They were curious at her finds in the playground. The hibernating ladybirds in a deep crevice in the wall or a spider spinning a web.

Lifting stones on the grass was fun and finding ants or other creepy-crawlies running about beneath them. Worms were a curiosity too, the way they burrowed into the soil and left worm casts.

She must have appeared strange to the other children, but she was very friendly and kind. She was independent and a very capable child. Any jobs the teacher wanted doing she always volunteered.

Her friends taught her the usual playground games. Hopscotch, whip and top, skipping, hide and seek, and tag.

As she got older, she cycled the two miles to school on her second-hand bicycle she'd received for her birthday.

Emily saw many things on the farm. Nipper, on one occasion, was sent into the barn after it had been sealed up. Her father had seen a rat run in and was determined to kill it.

He had his trousers tied with baler twine at the bottoms, to stop the rat running up his trouser legs. He had his large steel toe work boots on and carried a stick.

There was a lot of shrieking from both the dog and the rat as they fought to the death. Nipper came out victorious with a bloody nose.

"He's always been a good ratter," her father said, smiling, pleased he had killed the rat.

Emily was asked by her father to collect the metal bracket for the scythe's grip from the blacksmith, after school.

During playtime she saw her father driving the old grey Massey Ferguson tractor through the village. She assumed he had picked it up, so went home without it.

Her father was enraged when she returned home without it, deliberately disobeying him. He didn't wait for an explanation – he took his belt off and beat her.

Emily ran outside, and sobbed; she hated the world apart from her dear animals. She picked up her favourite hen and sat down, stroking it tenderly as she had often done, to calm herself down. Her hand gently stroked its neck and down the brown feathers on its back.

"Emily, Emily, come and feed the pet lamb," shouted her mother. Emily took the feeding bottle of milk from her hand and went into the shed where the lamb lay on some straw.

"Poor little thing," she murmured. "I'm sorry your mummy died, here is some milk." The lamb got up and she placed the teat in its mouth. She tipped the bottle upwards. Once it tasted milk it started to suck and its little tail wagged from side to side excitedly.

Her parents' abuse continued; she seemed to get the blame for everything in those days. Her mother was always shouting at her and many times she was slapped across the face. Sometimes she didn't even know what for.

Her father always seemed to be in a bad mood. She suffered occasional beatings from his belt. Only her animals kept her going and her friends at school.

She was only seven years old, when she was told to stand in the gap between the shed and the outside toilet building. Her father was moving some cattle and didn't want them escaping through the gap.

She stood there with a stick in each hand extended out to fill the gap. In the most frightening voice, she could muster she shouted, "Yah, Yah."

One bullock broke loose and started to run towards her; she was terrified. It looked huge. She worried she would get trampled to death, so ran behind the shed.

All the bullocks turned and ran after the first one, which was kicking its heels up in excitement. Her father was furious with her and got his belt unbuckled to lash out at her but she had run away into the meadow.

Emily kept a low profile for a few days as best she could. She hated upsetting anyone but seemed to manage to upset her parents most days.

She had to help her mother every winter in the attic. Snow would blow in through tiny holes between the roof slates, creating small piles of snow on the attic floor. Lime was mixed with water to plug the gaps.

When she was 10 years old, she was given a black Fell pony. She named her Melody. Her father seemed to enjoy lunging the pony on a long rope attached to the bit on the bridle.

It reminded him of his youth, when work horses did all the farm work instead of tractors. He used to break in the gentle giants and get them used to harness and the shafts. He spent hours with the work horses – it was his passion in life as a young man.

Emily held tightly onto the reins and the mane, riding bareback, her legs gripping the sides of the pony. She learned to stay on easily at a walk, but increasing the pace to a trot, she found it uncomfortable, bobbing up and down, at that pace.

"Lean back and stretch your legs forward; it will be better for you," was her father's advice. Emily fell off numerous times but was so keen to learn she would immediately get back on again.

After a few months Emily was enjoying the gentle rolling motion of the canter. She loved it. She was confident enough to ride Melody in the yard on her own. Walking and trotting her in circles and figure of eights, bareback.

"When can we get a saddle, Dad?" she asked excitedly.

"I'll try and pick a second-hand one up at the auction soon," he replied quite cheerfully.

Her father seemed to have mellowed over the last year. He no longer beat her with his belt but sometimes he would shout at her. Her mother, on the other hand, was always shouting at her for something or other.

After work and supper, evenings were spent in the sitting room. They had no mains electricity – the overhead cable would come later. They relied on a small generator which was in the stone shed. It was mainly for the electric lights.

Her father would read the newspaper and smoke cigarettes in his favourite armchair, or visit the local pub. Her mother would mend clothes or make peg rugs or knit.

Emily would help cut up old clothes with sharp scissors into four-inch lengths, making them two inches wide, to make the peg rugs.

Her mother would use a wooden peg to force the material through the weave of the hessian sacking and then through another hole. So, both ends appeared on the same side. It took hundreds of strips to complete the rug.

The rugs were heavy and hard wearing, in an array of colours. Emily had one near her bed which was in different shades of blue.

Nipper would lie snoring on the hearth peg rug, which was in various shades of brown. Emily's mother made most of their clothes. Sewing up dresses and knitting cardigans and jumpers in her spare time.

"The devil finds work for idle hands," she used to say.

Emily was expected to do more jobs outside, particularly at haymaking. The bales were too heavy for her to lift, so she had to roll them into the middle of the field, so they could be lifted onto the trailer with a hay fork.

Her mother would drive the tractor and her father would do the lifting. His brother would generally stack the trailer with the bales. The two brothers shared their hay making machinery as it was only needed once a year.

A group of teenagers would come from the village and help too. They didn't get paid, but they were well fed. Margaret would bring out a large tea pot full of tea and a basket full of baking, cheese or boiled eggs and bread rolls.

They would all sit on the hay bales and enjoy their feast. The smell of the hay in the sunshine, and the bright blue sky above was as good as going on holiday for the lads.

The stacked trailer was then secured by a cart rope, ready for the journey to the barn. They all would sit on top of the stack, for the ride home to unload it.

When Emily was young, she sat beside her mother on the tractor, in a secure box made by her father. Her father always mowed the grass with a cutter bar mower, for hay.

Her mother would drive the tractor with the Wuffler. It stirred the cut grass and fluffed it up so it would dry better. She also rowed up the dried grass with another machine ready for the baler.

Her mother would sing nursery rhymes with Emily and teach her the alphabet and numbers up to a hundred. It kept Emily occupied and awake. The smell of warm diesel and oil always reminded Emily of those happy summer days.

Emily also had to help drive the sheep to the river. The pool was used to dip the sheep to clear them of infestations of external parasites.

At shearing time, Emily helped pass the fleeces onto a board where they were spread out and any soiled wool removed.

The flanks of the fleece were folded into the centre and then it was tightly rolled up from the tail to the neck end. The neck fleece was firmly tucked into the fleece.

The bundle of wool was thrown into the large wool sack which was suspended from a beam with ropes. When it was full, Emily would be lifted in, to trample the wool down so that the sack could be sewn up. A large curved sack needle and string were used.

She loved the farming year: there was always something different happening every day. Lambing was her favourite time. She also loved to watch the lambs skipping and running about as they got older.

When she was about 11 years old, they suffered a very harsh winter. There was a lot of snow that year. The tractor and bucket were used to clear the four foot of snow in the yard.

They lost about thirty ewes under a snow drift. They had gone to shelter near a stone wall and the snow covered them, eventually suffocating them.

Ben, the sheep dog, saved a lot of the other sheep. He ran along the wall, then dug with his paws, showing them where to dig.

Between them they had managed to dig a lot out and lifted them out by their curled horns, some barely alive.

Emily worked so hard; she didn't want any of them to suffer. Cold, wet and exhausted, she struggled with her parents to lift them out of their frozen tomb.

Two of the kittens also froze to death that winter; they had been trapped outside. They were still sat together upright just as they had been when still alive.

Nature can be so cruel at times, she thought, a tear trickling down her face. At least the cattle had survived in the field barn. Only their water troughs had frozen. They had plenty of hay to eat.

Melody, her pony, was put to work carrying water and hay in her homemade harness and panniers, she could go where a tractor couldn't manage.

In the summer Nipper died at the grand old age of sixteen years. Emily was heartbroken – he had been a very faithful friend and was always there for her in her sad moments to comfort her.

Her father buried him in the meadow. Emily said a little prayer and placed a bunch of wildflowers on his grave.

On her fourteenth birthday she was given a sheep dog; she called him Jet. She spent hours training him to drive and round up a few sheep in the yard. She even learned to whistle instructions.

Emily was now an expert at laying the fires in the sitting room and in the range. The old newspapers were scrunched up and put into the grate, and kindling sticks would be laid across.

A large log was placed at the front of the fire and coal tipped behind. The match was struck and held downwards so the flame got a good hold.

The paper corners jutting out from the front grill were lit – it didn't take long before the paper and wood were alight with flames, heating up the coal which eventually burst into flames.

She was a good cook too and also baked cakes, buns and bread at the weekends. She wasn't interested in school. It was so boring compared to her life on the farm, but she did excel in sports and anything to do with nature.

She would do her homework in her bedroom, Jet by her side. Her father allowed Jet to live in the house to replace Nipper. It was company for Emily.

Jet would sleep at the end of her bed at night. Ben the experienced sheep dog and Jet would sometimes work together gathering in the sheep.

Emily was learning to drive the tractor now. She took over the driving her mother usually did at hay time.

Her father was keen for Emily to leave school at fifteen so he could expand the business. Emily agreed as she didn't like school anyway.

She wasn't paid a wage – she had her board and lodgings and pocket money, plus Melody and Jet's keep. She was expected to make her own clothes and still help in the house.

She worked long hours as her father was working more hours at the slaughter house. Besides the routine work with the animals; there were always fences to mend and parts of dry-stone walls to rebuild, after they had tumbled down.

Thistles and nettles growing in the fields were always a problem – she would use the scythe to mow them down. The pot holes in the farm road were constantly needing attention too.

There were sheds to muck out into the muck spreader linked onto the tractor. She would drive it into the field and spread the muck on the land in frosty weather. She would wallpaper and paint the sitting room during the winter months.

There was a dance in Canley at the Town Hall. It would be Emily's first dance, outside of school, at the age of sixteen. She had made an outfit especially for the occasion. A green skirt with white polka dots and matching top.

She was very excited about going. Her old schoolfriend Jill was accompanying her, and Jill's mother drove them there.

THE CHARMER

The music blared out, 'Good Day Sunshine,' by the Beatles. Some of the young girls were dancing together in groups, and boys of all ages stood by, staring at their movements – twisting and shaking. Arms waving and legs swinging.

The noise was deafening to Emily, but she was enjoying herself immensely. She saw an older lad watching her intently from the corner of her eye.

He had noticed her tall, slim body, curving and weaving through her dance movements. It had excited him. He watched her long dark chestnut hair flowing loose on her shoulders and her healthy ruddy cheeks and cherry lips.

He confidently came over and introduced himself.

"You move well," he said, embarrassing her. "I'm Neil, do you want to dance with me?"

Emily gasped in surprise. He grabbed her hand and lightly pulled her over to another area of the room. They danced together for the rest of the evening.

At the end of the last dance, he stroked her beautiful hair and cupped her face in his large warm hands and lovingly kissed her on her lips. It was her first kiss and she felt she would melt away in that very moment.

Emily was still glowing the following morning at breakfast.

"I can see that you had a good time last night," her mother teased. Emily grinned, her eyes twinkling mischievously.

"Who did you dance with?" Her father asked inquisitively.

Emily's cheeks flushed slightly. "First of all, I danced with my old school friends. Then Neil asked me to dance."

"Neil Dale!" her Father said; he sounded a little surprised. Emily nodded.

"Well you won't get much better than Neil round here, mi lass."

Emily felt reassured he liked him.

Neil had arranged to ring Emily that night. She waited at the telephone box down the road from her farm; she was so pleased when he rang.

He wanted to take her out in his car to Farnton for a walk at the weekend. Her father agreed, as long as they got home before dark.

Emily couldn't wait to see him again – she had not received so much loving attention since she was a young child.

The weekend finally came and she was being driven in his Hillman Minx. She felt so grown up. Neil chatted away to her continuously, telling her all about his farm.

They parked on a grassy verge. He turned to her and gave her a kiss on her cheek.

"Come on, I'll race you to the top of the hill," he said, scrambling out of the car as fast as he could.

He had already vaulted the five barred gate before Emily had run around the car. She chased after him up the hill, determined to beat him.

Her strides were no match for his longer strides. When she reached him at the top of the hill, he swung her round in his muscular arms.

She felt as if she was flying like a bird in the sky. He then kissed her passionately. Her big brown eyes looked up at his sunburnt face and she knew then that he was the one.

They went out a lot that summer and spent many happy hours together. Her father would meet up with Neil at the pub sometimes, in Townsfoot, Finley or Canley. They would talk all about farming and arrange to share and swap machinery.

Brian was treating Neil like a son; he had always wanted a son. When his wife, Margaret, could not conceive again, after Emily, he felt frustrated and blamed

Margaret. This spilled over onto poor Emily in her early years, as she was not as capable as a boy.

Emily and Jill went to Canley on the Saturday to do some shopping. They visited the cafe for a cup of tea and cakes. Emily excitedly told Jill all about her boyfriend Neil.

"Be careful, Emily," she warned. "He has played the field and dumped a lot of girls; he is only after one thing."

"All men sow their wild oats before they settle down," she retorted. "He's been different with me; I think he is ready to settle down and is treating me like a lady."

"Don't you think he is a bit old for you?" Jill said, thinking he would be an old man long before Emily would be old.

"He's ten years older than me. I know a lot of relationships that work where there is an age difference, particularly in the farming community," Emily replied, strongly defending the scenario.

"If you are happy with him then I'm happy for you. I hope you get married and experience married bliss – it's every girl's dream." Jill laughed.

Emily's cheeks flushed as she joined her friend laughing. Emily told her she had been invited to see his farm. Up to now, Neil had always been to her house or taken her out.

"Every time he comes to supper, he brings my mum a bunch of flowers! Mum would giggle and say 'what a charmer you are'. She was quite tickled by the attention really, I've never seen her acting so girly before," Emily told her friend.

"Yes, he does sound like the real charmer," Jill said grinning.

"He always brings me something too. Last week he brought me this chain and locket." Emily produced the gift from under the neckline of her yellow jumper.

Jill looked at it enviously. Emily's name was engraved on the front.

"What have you put inside it?"

"Nothing yet," was the reply. "What should I put in it?" Emily quizzed.

Jill pondered for a while, twisting her hair in her fingers.

"The key to his heart," came the reply.

Emily was confused. "What do you mean?"

Jill laughed. "Do you have an old suitcase key? You could put it in your locket and fantasise it's the key that will open his heart to you." They both laughed at the notion.

That night Emily rummaged around and found a small key from her old toy jewellery box. This will do, she thought and tucked it into the sterling silver locket. She held the locket tightly in both hands, wishing that she would one day marry Neil.

When Emily went to see Neil's farm, she fell in love with it immediately. When he had told her about it, he had described the farm as if it was ready to fall down. So, she was pleasantly surprised.

The farmhouse was a lot bigger than her own. The kitchen was modern with a free-standing cooker and grill.

The cupboards where fitted and there was a stainless-steel sink. A twin tub washing machine stood in the corner. It was so modern compared to what she was used to.

There was a door leading to the walk-in pantry similar to the one at home. There was a long lounge with a television and a splendid dining room, although most meals were eaten in the kitchen.

Upstairs there were three good sized bedrooms and a modern bathroom.

"Do you like my house?" Neil inquired.

Emily looked up at him grinning. "It's a beautiful house, I love it."

Neil kissed her lightly on the forehead, and gently led her into his bedroom. He laid her down on the soft quilt spread over his bed. Emily's mind was not just flying in the sky now but in the stars.

Neil caressed her lovingly, his hand slowly slid down her side and under her dress. Emily was not sure about this; it was happening too quick.

The phone rang loudly from the landing outside. Neil jumped off the bed to answer it. He remembered he was expecting a call from the vet.

Emily quietly slipped away down into the lounge. Later Neil walked in, looking a bit sheepish.

"Sorry, Emily, I got a bit carried away there." He held her body tight to his. "I do love you. . .very much."

"I've loved you since the day you swung me around on the hill," Emily declared softly. She had never been so happy.

Jill and Emily met for their usual afternoon shopping in Canley and went to the cafe. They caught up on their news.

Then Jill began to fidget uneasily before she blurted out, "I don't want to upset you, Emily but I saw Neil with another girl in Townsfoot. He was talking to her intently and gave her a kiss on her forehead."

Emily was shocked – was it because he didn't get his way with her and was now looking elsewhere?

"I can't believe he would do that after saying he loved me very much." She began to cry quietly. Jill comforted her the best she could.

"When did he say he would see you again?" she asked.

"He is supposed to be ringing me up tonight to the telephone box." Emily replied, wiping away her tears.

"Then you'll know if he still wants you," was Jill's answer to the predicament.

Emily waited at the telephone box at the arranged time. There was no phone call. She waited in the cold for an hour hoping and praying he would ring.

She walked home utterly miserable. Sunken in grief that their romance had ended.

"What are you looking so miserable about?" her mother asked, when Emily got home.

Emily walked past her, saying, "nothing, Mum." She walked up to her bedroom. Jet got up from the rug and followed her.

She lay on her bed and sobbed. Jet whined and laid his paw on her, trying to comfort her. Emily sat up suddenly, took out the key from the locket and wished as hard as she could for Neil to come back

The following evening, they heard a car drive up to the front door.

"Who could that be this time of night," her father moaned. "Margaret, see who it is."

Emily could hear the voice at the door and knew it was Neil. Was he coming to 'dump her' like Jill said he did to all his girlfriends? she wondered.

He entered the room with a beautiful bunch of flowers.

"I'm so sorry, Emily," he began, "there was an emergency yesterday at the farm and I couldn't phone you." He handed the flowers to her and smiled.

"We had a cow having a very bad calving, I had to get the vet. We were very late milking."

Emily didn't know what to say or think. She offered him a mug of tea and they both went into the kitchen away from her parents.

Neil chattered away as usual as if nothing was going on. Emily wanted to know so much – had Jill really seen him with another girl?

"You're quiet tonight, what's up, are you still mad at me?" Neil asked, wondering why she looked upset.

Emily had already made the tea and arranged the flowers in a vase. She plucked up the courage to ask, "Who was the girl you were seen with in Townsfoot?"

Neil laughed. "Is that what all the misery is about?" He drew her close to him and continued, "She is my cousin Ann, her pony had just dropped dead of red worm infestation that morning and I was trying to comfort her."

Emily was so relieved; it took all her strength not to cry with all the emotions she had been dealing with. She smiled, and Neil kissed her affectionately on her cheek.

Emily embraced him enthusiastically, her doubts and suspicions all melted away. Emily started chatting cheerfully until he had to go.

Christmas Dinner was arranged at Emily's house for Neil. He brought presents for everyone. Margaret received a brooch, which she was delighted with. Brian was given a farmer's carved stick for his days at the auction.

Emily received a silver bracelet with his name engraved and intertwined with hers. She was overwhelmed by it – he certainly knew how to spoil her.

Emily had knitted him a thick woolly jumper and scarf. Neil enjoyed being with her family – he missed his own family terribly.

Neil and Emily brought in the New Year, 1968, together. They had gone to a dance in Townsfoot. Brian didn't worry anymore about her being home late. He completely trusted Neil to bring her back safely.

Emily's birthday was in the January, she was 17 years old. Neil gave her a large sewing box which stood on carved legs, a lovely piece of furniture. The lid lifted and the side trays folded out revealing plenty of space below. She adored it.

In the early spring, Neil and Brian were supping pints in the pub at Canley together and discussing the farming year ahead. Then Brian changed the subject abruptly.

"Don't you think it's about time you and Emily got engaged?"

There was an awkward pause in the conversation.

"I've thought about it...a lot as a matter of fact," Neil responded.

"Well get on with it, lad," Brian urged. "Emily will make you a good wife. She is hard working and a good cook. She'll tackle any farming job."

Neil didn't know whether he was worthy of her. He had had a wild time after his parents died. Emily, on the other hand, was so pure and innocent, he thought.

"I'll get around to it one day, when the time is right," Neil said encouragingly.

One beautiful spring day, Emily and Neil were taking it in turns to ride Melody on a walk up into the hills. Jet followed on behind.

Emily was showing him the land they rented and the breath-taking views from the hills. They sat down together on the rough grass.

Neil asked her if she ever wanted to get married. Emily was shocked and wondered if he was going to propose there and then. Her face coloured up.

"Of course, it's every girl's wish to get married and have a family of her own," she said.

"And what about you?" Emily asked curiously.

"I'm not proud of my past, I've done things I deeply regret. I've hurt people's feelings in my crazy past. That what's stopping me ever getting married."

"Surely, you have learnt from that and grown up and moved on? It's what life is all about," Emily gently reassured him.

He changed the subject and no more was said about it as they returned home.

Emily was very busy with lambing for a couple of weeks and did not get chance to see Neil. She received a couple of letters from him in the post. He was a real charmer at writing too. She loved to receive his letters; it would add a sparkle and lift to her day.

She would write after she had eaten supper. She couldn't write as well as he did but she always signed off, 'Love Emily xxx'.

She longed to be in his arms again, it was almost painful, the ache she felt inside her. She dearly hoped he would eventually ask her to marry him and then they would be together for ever.

Neil arrived one evening unexpectedly. "I thought I would surprise you."

Emily was thrilled. "It's so good to see you, come on in, we will go into the kitchen."

They talked about lambing time and what Neil had been doing on his farm.

"I have the chance to go to Canada for three months. My uncle will look after the farm with the staff."

Emily's heart sank. She couldn't bear the thought of them being apart for so long and Neil so far away.

"Do you really want to go?" asked Emily shocked at his news.

"It's a chance of a lifetime," he told her excitedly. "I'll be able to learn such a lot."

Emily cast her eyes down at the floor; he wasn't even thinking about us, she thought.

"Before I go, I want to ask you something," he said, lifting her chin and looking into her sad eyes. "Will you be faithful to me and wait for my return?"

"Of course, I will, of course I will!" Emily flung her arms around him tightly – she didn't want to let him go.

"Then will you marry me, Emily?" Neil asked, speaking softly.

Emily's big brown eyes lit up, and she laughed.

Her emotions had swung from one extreme to another that night.

"Yes, yes I would dearly love to marry you."

Neil pulled out of his pocket, a small leather box. He opened it carefully and removed a cluster diamond ring. He placed it on Emily's finger.

Emily looked lovingly at him and at her ring – she couldn't believe they were finally engaged. They embraced and kissed. It was magical to her and she felt their souls were finally one.

Neil asked her, "I thought we could have the wedding in October at your Parish Church – what do you think?"

Emily was so excited. "It sounds wonderful."

She ran into the sitting room. "Look, look, we're engaged!" she excitedly told her parents, showing off her ring.

"About time too," Brian joked, jumping to his feet. He hugged Emily and then shook Neil's hand.

Her mother grinned and laughed. "Congratulations, both of you. When is the wedding?"

They told her their plans and the rest of the evening was spent discussing the dress and bridesmaids. Neil was going to ask his cousin Len to be the best man.

Emily lay in bed that night smiling. Her life was going to dramatically change and for the better, she thought. A loving husband, a lovely house and a farm too. She felt so lucky.

Her parents were in bed discussing the finances for the coming wedding.

"I hope he doesn't find another girl in Canada and call off the wedding!" Margaret whispered.

"He'll have me to answer to, if he does!" Brian said crossly. "I'm not forking out all this dosh for nowt."

Neil arrived home to his farm. He looked into the calving shed to see if all was well with a cow. He eventually slid into bed. He was a bit amazed at himself, for finally making the big move forward. It had been on his mind for some time.

There was still some doubt as to whether he had done the right thing – he enjoyed being a bachelor and the freedom that came with it.

Neil and Emily had a couple of months together before Neil would go to Canada.

Emily was determined to spend every spare moment with him.

They spent a lot of time at Neil's farm on her days off. On one occasion Emily was leaning over the half door to the calving shed, admiring the view of the green fields, hedges and dry-stone walls.

Neil was shaking out clean straw from the bale he had just brought in. He was expecting a cow to calve soon and would be bringing her in later.

He approached Emily from behind and hugged her affectionately. His hands slid under her jumper, he caressed her warm body and cupped his hands around her breasts.

Emily cherished every second. Neil gently swung her round and kissed her passionately. They tumbled onto the straw and rolled together tightly.

"Neil, Neil," shouted a loud male voice. It was the cowman, Greg.

Neil got up in a hurry and brushed himself down.

"I'm coming," he said, a little annoyed.

Emily had also scrambled to her feet and tried to get the straw out of her jumper and hair.

Greg had got the cow in the yard and wanted a turn with it, into the shed. It was showing the calf's feet: the calf was nearly ready to be born.

On their last evening together, Neil lit a fire in the lounge fireplace. Emily came in with hot drinks on a tray. She set it down on the coffee table.

"I don't know what I'll do with myself when you're gone," Emily sighed, sitting down on the settee.

Neil sat beside her and held her hand. "Remember you are always in my heart, I've never felt like this with anyone else, you are definitely the one for me."

They kissed tenderly and caressed; he was sending ripples of excitement through her body. The fire was ablaze now, spreading out a warm glow to the room.

Neil gently guided her to the sheepskin rug nearer the fire and they lay down in each other's loving arms. Emily felt ready this time.

She loved his adorable little touches and kisses on her neck and his warm lips on hers.

His warm breath on her tummy bringing amazing feelings rushing through her veins. He was so gentle and smooth in his affectionate moves over her body.

She felt helpless under his loving spell. Finally, the enchanting, heavenly crescendo of emotions rocked her very being. She was in heaven! She bathed in the glorious intensity of the moment.

Neil gently rolled off her body, cuddling her at his side. Both were breathing heavily and perspiration glistened on their foreheads. It had been ecstasy for them both.

Emily knew the wonderful experience would give her strength, through the lonely days before her. Neil knew she was his truly beloved one.

Emily met Jill again in Canley; she couldn't wait to show off her diamond ring.

"I'm so jealous, what a beautiful ring," Jill exclaimed, touching the glittering diamonds, her eyes shining with happiness for her.

Emily told her all about their plans and about Neil's Canadian trip.

"Well, he has certainly made sure you will not look at another man while he is away."

Emily told her they had made love on the last night. The mere thought of the memories brought back the excitement and that heavenly feeling ascended through her body.

Jill was caught up in the rush of excitement of her friend and started asking lots of questions. Emily's face reddened.

"I'll tell you one day but not now," she said.

Her friend felt deflated – she was just getting interested.

"Will you be my bridesmaid, Jill?" Emily asked, hoping her best friend would be available for the big occasion.

"You bet, I wouldn't miss it for the world," was her resounding reply.

They visited the Bridal Shop just for a peep. Jill found a dress she really liked.

"I could make that for a fraction of the price," Emily gasped. "I will probably wear my mum's wedding dress, with a few alterations and a few things to alter the design a bit."

Emily absorbed herself into the work on her farm and the wedding preparations, to prevent herself from over thinking about Neil. Her days off were particularly lonely – she spent the time with Melody and Jet, riding the country lanes and into the hills.

It was great excitement to receive Neil's long love letters. She would read them over and over, bewitched by every word.

She would write back with equally long letters, but always felt she couldn't ever get that same romantic vibe as Neil could.

NEIL GROWING UP

Neil thought deeply about the events of his life as he travelled to Canada. In contrast to Emily's life, Neil had been born into a wealthy family in 1941 at Meadows Farm.

His parents doted on him and spoilt him. He was given his own way a lot of the time. He had lots of toys growing up, many from relations.

Toy factories had been taken over for the war effort, so many of his toys were homemade wooden soldiers and tanks. A wooden cart with pram and bicycle wheels was his favourite, and farm animals carved out of wood.

His father made him a model aircraft out of balsa wood covered with tissue. The powering mechanism was a large length of heavy-duty elastic to power the propeller.

His mother didn't work on the farm – she had trained as a primary school teacher and wasn't the least bit interested in animals or the farm. She hated getting dirty.

Before Neil was born, she spent her time entertaining their wealthy friends, shopping and having her hair done every week. She had a part-time maid in the house as she hated housework.

Her husband would often accompany her to shows and the theatre. They joined friends for dinner at expensive hotels and to their friends' houses for parties.

Neil's father had inherited the farm from his father. He enjoyed farming, but generally spent his time supervising the farm staff and playing golf.

The war broke out in 1939 and the golf course was taken over for the war effort to grow food. Their flamboyant lifestyles were also curbed. His mother would instead attend clubs for the war effort. There were rationing and blackouts to cope with.

Food was plentiful on the farm, not like the shortages in the cities. Neil's family had their own hens laying eggs, milk from the cows and the staff tended a vegetable and fruit garden.

The farm had its own orchard. They had a beef herd and a lambing flock so there was plenty of beef and lamb to eat. There were also rabbits to shoot and mushrooms to pick in the fields.

The maid was called up for active service but failed her medical so she had to work in the Mental Hospital in Townsfoot. Neil's mother employed a fifteen-year-old girl as another maid to help her in the house.

Neil's early memories were the blackout curtains hung at his bedroom window. The room was pitch black at night. Sometimes he would hear the hum of the aircraft above. He was never afraid.

He could remember his mother's old gramophone with the handle at the side to wind it up. Her favourite records were of Gracie Fields. He often listened to them, sat on his mother's knee.

On one occasion, there was an aircraft flying towards Finley, obviously having problems. Most people had heard the engines spluttering, and saw the smoke streaming out of the engine. Some had observed the aircraft's right wing dipped and not flying level.

People prayed it would not crash into the school as it noisily approached. Mothers screamed and cried helplessly as they watched it drawing near.

It was obvious the aircraft would come down as it was in so much difficulty. It appeared it was trying to avoid crashing into the village. It was a relief when it missed the school.

The pilot and crew died as heroes and were praised for their ultimate bravery in steering the aircraft away from the village to their deaths.

"They must have known what they were doing, and knew they would not come out of it alive," a mother cried, so grateful for their sacrifice.

Neil remembered the loud bang. He had looked out of his bedroom window. Smoke and flames poured out from the wreckage of the aircraft, which had crashed into one of their perimeter fields.

He ran downstairs as everyone piled onto the tractor and trailer to see if there were any survivors. He was lifted onto the trailer; he thought it was all wonderfully exciting.

The flames were too intense to get anywhere near the plane. They stood back in case it exploded.

The outline of the tail was stuck in the air at an angle, towering above him. The nose and cockpit were crumpled and embedded into the ground.

"It's one of ours," exclaimed Frank, the stockman. There was a strong smell of aviation fuel in the air and the acrid smell of smoke from the burning rubber tyres.

They all felt helpless stood there not being able to do anything.

"Probably a couple of lads on a training exercise, poor souls. What a waste," Neil's father lamented.

Neil didn't feel any emotions – as a small boy of three years old, he didn't really understand. It was an exhilarating adventure to him.

He would re-enact the scene many times with his toy aircraft not really realising the full implications of the disaster to the crew killed and their families.

Finley had been far removed from the horrors of war until then. They had not experienced any bombings like London and elsewhere.

Neil vaguely remembered his mother looking after evacuees. They were a lot older than him and had started at the grammar school in Townsfoot. They were in their room at night doing homework so he didn't remember having much to do with them.

In 1947, the winter was very severe. It was extremely cold with lots of snow. Neil was only six years of age. He would play out in the snow, building little snowmen and throwing snowballs at the farm staff.

He remembered, he had run through some snow and disappeared from view. He had run across a ditch and the snow gave way. He returned home wet and very cold. His mother gave him a warm bath in front of the open fire to warm him up.

At a young age Neil showed arrogance and he was a bully. He would boss around his younger cousins Len and Ann, who often stayed during holidays. His mother loved other children around her.

Len and Neil would play tricks on Ann. One time, they had prepared a toffee tin under her bed with a cotton reel in it. They carefully reeled out the cotton to their room where the boys slept.

That night while Ann was in bed, the two boys pulled at the cotton. The cotton reel spun around and rattled in the tin, disturbing Ann.

She ran into the boys' room across the landing. She was very afraid – she thought the bogey man was coming to get her. The boys laughed and laughed. Ann wasn't very pleased and began to cry.

The farm was ideal for the children to play in, lots of space to run and hide. Len and Neil would often play at being soldiers. They had wooden rifles and would pretend to be in battles.

Ann would pretend to be a devoted nurse. She would dutifully run around and when one of them acted dead she would touch them on the arm to bring them back to life, for the battle to continue.

Once when Len was ill in bed, Neil, now nine years of age, took Ann to the barn.

"I bet you can't climb those ladders onto the loft," Neil told Ann.

"Bet I can," came the determined reply.

"Alright, I'll help you," Neil coaxed, following her up the ladder. Ann was quite relieved when she arrived at the top – she didn't particularly enjoy climbing the ladder.

"Now you wait there while I go down first," Neil explained, descending the ladder. When he arrived at the bottom, he deliberately pushed the ladder away, leaving poor Ann stranded.

Neil thought it was a huge joke, but six-year-old Ann began to cry. Neil laughed and ran away. Ann started screaming in distress, until finally the cowman, Greg, got her down.

Neil was later reprimanded by his father but nothing more was said. That same summer Neil got Ann to go to the meal house with him. He amused her by climbing into a large empty meal bin.

"I want to come in too," she begged. Neil laughed.

"You're too small to climb in here with me. Should I help you?"

"Yes," replied Ann enthusiastically, "here is my hand."

She managed to climb into the bin with Neil's help and sat down with him. They played with the marbles that Neil had in his pocket.

Neil knew Ann's parents would be coming to collect her soon. He would enjoy the commotion when they couldn't find her.

"Shush, now, Ann, let's pretend there are bad men after us and we have to be very quiet."

It took Ann's parents, Neil's parents and the farm staff an hour to find them. Neil thought it was a great joke. He was told off by his father for wasting everyone's time but Neil didn't care. He was never slapped or beaten; his parents didn't believe in it.

Neil was attending a small private day school, called Rook Park. His parents wanted him to have a good education. He had left the infants at the village school when he turned seven years old.

He was a bright boy and excelled in all his subjects. He was always the leader in his group. He was an extrovert and loved to organise his classmates at playtime.

He had a furious temper, if he didn't get his own way. He got into a lot of fights. He was very defiant. If he chose not to eat his dinner, the staff could not persuade him otherwise.

The Head Master would send him into the kitchen to stay until he ate it. It never worked: Neil would rather starve to death than give in to anyone.

He knew how to get his own way with his mother. He learnt how to charm her with compliments or pick flowers for her. She thought he was the 'bee's knees' and absolutely adored her only son.

His mother and the maid waited on him hand and foot. When he got undressed, he would just drop his clothes on the floor. Someone else was expected to tidy up after him, including his toys.

As Neil turned ten years old, his father expected him to do a few jobs for his pocket money. He had to drive the hens into the hen house at night – if they didn't get in quick enough, he would lash out with his foot.

He would tease the sheep dog by placing his dish of food just out of reach from the length of chain, to see how he would react.

The dog would try his best to reach his dinner, whining and scratching. Neil would then kick the bowl nearer and watch the dog wolf down his food.

When Ann came to visit, Neil offered her a cup of tea. He had laced it with salt just to see how she reacted. The first sip was immediately spat out. Ann lashed out at him with her tiny fist, but Neil was too quick and ran away.

What Neil did to others, he thought was all a huge joke – he didn't understand he was upsetting people.

As he got older, he lost his respect for his mother. He would criticise her about the way she looked or how she did things. His mother never stood up to him. She thought he could do no wrong.

His father had a temper but never laid a hand on him. He would shout at him and order him to his room when Neil was naughty.

Neil was given an Arab pony – he called him Blaze after the white marking on its face. He soon learnt to ride and entered children's pony shows. He always expected to win and had a tantrum if he didn't.

He later passed his entrance exam for the public school, at Ackworth House, an impressive building with a long straight drive leading up to the main double doors.

He boarded there until he was 18 years old. He hated it being so academic, and the discipline was strict, something he was not used to.

He played truant one summer's day – a friend joined him to go to the river for a swim. They stripped down to their underpants and dived in. They laughed and joked, splashing each other and generally having a good time.

His friend swam further out and got into difficulty, in the undercurrent. He suddenly disappeared from view. Neil was frantic, he didn't know what to do.

He tried to see if he would pop up further down the river. There was no sign of him. He raced to get help from nearby.

His friend's body was eventually pulled out later that day. The police interviewed Neil at the school with the Head Master present.

He was very nervous when questioned by the two police officers. He told them exactly what had happened and told them he was very sorry.

Neil was devastated and felt numb about his friend's death. He had prepared for the cane he knew he would receive. He had padded his underpants well.

"Bend over, boy. I hope these six lashes will teach you not to play truant." The Head Master then meted out his punishment.

Neil didn't feel much. He still felt traumatised and in a daze. The events of the day felt surreal to him – he couldn't believe it had all happened.

His parents were informed by telephone and by letter. His mother was very concerned for Neil. His father was furious with him for playing truant in the first place, allowing the death to happen.

At seventeen years old Neil lost interest in studying – his mind was more on girls. He was at an all-boys school so his attention turned to the female domestic staff.

He liked a girl about sixteen who worked in the kitchen; she loved to flirt with him. He would often steal a kiss when he could. His Head Master did not approve and banned him from the kitchen area.

He was made a prefect to give him some responsibility and to keep him occupied. He enjoyed the control. Anyone out of line, particularly the bullies, he would send them to the prefects' room.

The rest of the prefects would gather and choose a suitable punishment for the boys. One notorious young bully was degraded and humiliated by having to wear a dress and stand on a chair and sing nursery rhymes. He never bullied anyone again.

In Neil's final year, he was voted in as Head Boy as he was very popular amongst staff and pupils. He took his duties seriously and made his parents and the school very proud of him.

He achieved good grades and was accepted at Thorpe Hall Agricultural College. He enjoyed studying farm management at the college immensely – it was where his real interest lay in life.

His charismatic nature always drew friends around him – they would go off drinking and get blind drunk, driving recklessly back to college.

His mates took priority now more than girls, he had such a good time with them. They had Sundays off, so they would drive somewhere and camp out over Saturday night. They would sling a tarpaulin over a rope tied to two trees, and sleep under that.

They would bring plenty of bottled beer to drink. There were the usual dares and discussions about girls. When they were sober, they would go swimming and walking. He loved his time with his rowdy mates.

He managed to get his final qualifications from his College. Both his parents were very proud of him. He went to live at home to work on his father's farm. His father made him a full partner in the business.

Neil worked very hard; he appeared to have settled down and was well admired. He took on the managing of the local Young Farmers' Club. He was a star at debates and a good organiser in other clubs he joined.

He would enter competitions at the local show, ploughing matches, sheep dog trials and dry-stone walling events.

He would make a polite appearance at his parents' endless social events, garden parties, sherry mornings, cocktail parties and dinners.

His mother proudly showed off her son to her guests, mentioning he had been Head Boy and had been to college.

It wasn't really Neil's scene – he would rather be at the pub with his mates. He felt more relaxed with his own generation.

He was fast asleep in bed in the winter of 1965, when he woke to find his room lit up with a blue flashing light. Someone was knocking furiously at the front door. He jumped out of bed and opened the curtains. It was the police.

He thought some cows must have got out of the shed and wandered onto the road and the police were here to tell him. He put on his dressing gown and ran downstairs.

There were two police officers; they asked to come in to speak to him. Neil led them into the kitchen.

"I suggest you take a seat; we have some bad news for you," said one of the officers.

Neil knew then it was nothing to do with cattle escaping – they would have told him at the front door.

The police officer continued, "Your parents were involved in a car accident."

Neil's heart sank.

"They both died at the scene of the accident," they told him.

Neil didn't really hear anything after that. He felt totally stunned, his head bowed, he was speechless. It was unimaginable that a tragedy like this could have happened to his mum and dad. They were only in their fifties.

The police left after making him a mug of tea and offering to call someone for him. Neil just wanted to be left alone.

There was a very big turnout for the funeral, the church was overflowing into the grounds outside. Everywhere was festooned with flowers from everyone they knew.

People showed their sympathy and pity to Neil. His parents were buried side by side in the grave yard. Neil was glad when it was all over. He generally craved attention but not this sort.

Neil's uncle was a great support to him in those early days after the funeral. The farm generally ran well with the experienced staff; they all said they would stay on to work for Neil.

Neil's character changed: he hated how life had treated him. He often lashed out his pain on the world, by arguing with neighbours and friends.

He would throw hammers and spanners in a temper when he couldn't mend the machinery. He would lose patience with cows at milking time and lash out at them.

"He's like a bear with a sore head," his friends and staff would say. "He'll get over it in time."

Neil found comfort in drinking; he would often be late for milking the next day due to his hangovers. The staff patiently carried on without him, hoping he would get over his grief.

Neil would pick up flirtatious girls from dances and sleep around, then dump them unceremoniously. His emotional pain would only leave him briefly in these flings. He was getting a very bad reputation locally.

He befriended a homeless man called Joe Stokes, a twenty-two-year-old. He was tall and of average build, he was looking for casual work.

Neil offered him odd jobs repairing walls and fences, mowing down nettles and thistles. Also painting wooden gates with creosote and corrugated iron roofs with bitumen paint.

Joe stayed in an outbuilding with a bed and wardrobe. The light was controlled from a switch in the house. Neil made sure he went to sleep early so he got up in the morning as he was quite lazy.

Joe encouraged the vulnerable Neil in his drinking. In their drunken state, Joe egged Neil on to rustle sheep, using Neil's Land Rover and cattle trailer. Neil was always ready for a dare. Joe was wanting some easy money and Neil was his path towards it.

Neil split the money: Joe was only given thirty percent. Neil had provided the transport, fuel and housed the sheep before the sale, so he thought he was entitled to more.

They were both drunk again at the time. Joe became enraged and began to argue and became very aggressive. They fought furiously. Finally, Joe was flung backwards with an almighty punch from Neil into Joe's neck.

Joe lay motionless in the dirt. Neil gasped – what had he done? He shook Joe violently, but no response. He panicked; frantic he wondered what to do. His heart was racing, it was difficult to think.

He laid his jacket over Joe to help him keep warm. He thought he was just unconscious and would eventually come around, but deep down he knew he was dead.

Neil brought the Land Rover round. He bent down to feel his skin. It was going cold and was starting to mottle as his blood began to pool. Neil knew for sure he was dead.

He bungled the body into the back of the vehicle. He drove down to the wood and found a clearing. He buried him as deep as he could in the soft earth, but was hindered by the tree roots. He covered the site with rotting twigs and leaves to disguise the grave.

It was a big wake up call for Neil: he had blood on his hands now. He vowed he would straighten his life around and never get drunk again.

He got rid of Joe's sparse belongings by burning them on the open fire in his lounge. The next day, before the maid arrived, he picked out any buckles, studs and buttons left from the clothing and he threw them away.

Joe was missed that day by the staff.

"Where is Joe this morning?" Harold the tractor man asked. Neil told him to check the outbuilding.

Harold returned and told his boss, "He looks as if he's moved on, his belongings have gone. He won't be missed, he was a young scoundrel, if ever there was one."

"Best he's gone, I didn't get much work out of him," Neil replied. Joe was never mentioned again.

Neil flung himself into his farm work and tried to be a better person from then on. He felt guilt and remorse but was determined to put it all behind him.

People noticed the change and were pleased. They thought he had finally come out of his grief. He was starting to be respected again by the locals after his wild days.

He attended and supported charity events held in Finley and became the main organiser for the pony show.

He didn't entertain like his parents but was occasionally asked to open garden parties and attend dinners.

He became a Parish Councillor and worked diligently for the good of his Parish. It was a lot of work and meetings were generally held in an evening.

Neil completed his three months in Canada.

It was an experience he would never forget. He had stayed with his uncle's cousin on his farm. It was mainly growing wheat, oats and potatoes. He also spent time in forestry work nearby.

On his journey home, he thought about Emily. She wasn't like any other girl he had met. She was more down to earth and definitely more capable.

He truly loved her and was longing for the day to make her his wife and have lots of children.

He dearly wanted a boy to carry on the farm and the family name. He hoped Emily had stayed faithful to him and she had not changed her mind about the wedding.

THE WEDDING

"You're back!" screamed Emily, very excited. "Come on in."

Neil had arrived in the early morning at his farm. He caught up with sleep and visited Emily that evening.

Jet was there greeting him with licks and wagging his tail, curious to know what was in his bag.

Neil and Emily passionately hugged and kissed. Emily had longed for this moment. Neil was relieved she hadn't changed her love for him. It was as if they had never been apart.

He pulled a box out of his bag and handed it to her. Inside was a silver maple leaf brooch.

"Gosh, it's beautiful, thank you so much,"

Emily said excitedly. She wrapped her arms around him and kissed him.

"I haven't finished yet!" He pulled out a soft toy of a Canadian Mountie.

Emily laughed. "It's lovely." She looked at the detailed work of the red tunic and the Stetson hat with its wide flat brim. She loved it.

He was always spoiling her and it made her feel very special.

"I have presents for your parents – are they in the sitting room?"

"No, they have gone out but will be back soon."

They sat and chatted in the sitting room. Neil was enthusiastically telling her all about his adventures in Canada.

Emily told him about the wedding arrangements that had been made, and that Jill was going to be her bridesmaid. They arranged to spend her next day off at his farm.

A car drew up into the yard. It was her parents arriving home. They had seen Neil's car and burst into the house, thrilled to bits he had arrived home safely from Canada.

Brian poured Neil a beer and Margaret fetched in some homemade cakes to eat. They all talked excitedly at once.

Neil handed them their presents. A souvenir Canadian plate for Margaret and a matching ash tray for Brian.

They were both pleased and felt he was such a good lad for their daughter to marry. Neil enjoyed being in the family group – he still missed his own mum and dad very much.

Neil picked up Emily in his car on her day off as arranged. It was a lovely sunny day for the end of September, the trees were changing colour into beautiful shades of reds and browns. It was not long now to the wedding.

Neil had missed hay making and harvest on his own farm. His uncle had seen to the supervision of staff and they had had a good summer and bumper crops.

They arrived at Meadows Farm. Neil led her into his house. They ran into the lounge and held each other very close.

"Promise you will never leave me again, it was torture," Emily said softly.

Neil kissed her gently on her warm lips and quietly responded, "I'll never leave you again, promise. I'll always be here for you forever. I can't wait till you are my wife."

Emily grinned; she couldn't wait either to be by his side for ever. Neil lowered her onto the sheepskin rug.

There was a sudden slam of a door. Neil heard the maid in the kitchen starting to prepare a meal.

"Oh no, I forgot she was coming in today," Neil remarked, disappointed. They got up and sat on the settee together, holding hands.

Neil suddenly felt unwell. His head began to spin, his vision was blurred and he felt hot. He tried to stand but collapsed on the floor as his legs buckled beneath him.

"Help, help," Emily screamed. The maid rushed in.

"Whatever is the matter, what's wrong with him?" the maid cried out, rushing to Neil's side. "He's got a high temperature, I'll ring the doctor," she told Emily.

Emily tried to make him comfortable – he was too heavy for her to help sit him on the settee so she waited for the maid to return to help her.

The doctor arrived and examined him. "You look as if you have caught the flu on your travels," he informed him, returning his stethoscope back into his black bag. He continued, "Have plenty of bed rest, drink plenty of fluids and eat well to keep your strength up."

The doctor stood up and looked down at him. "If you are no better in about five days call me." Emily thanked the doctor and the maid showed him out.

Emily and the middle-aged maid struggled to help him upstairs to his room. The maid left to return to making the meal in the kitchen. Emily helped Neil undress and get him into bed.

He was grateful she was there to help him. He felt very tired and weak; he just wanted to sleep. The jet lag didn't help either.

Emily arranged for the maid to look after him the following day. Harold, the tractor man drove Emily home that night in Neil's car.

Emily and her parents, hoped he would make a full recovery for his wedding day on Saturday 12th October, or else everything would have to be cancelled and all the invitations had already gone out.

Emily phoned Neil's house from the telephone box down the road the following day. The maid answered and told her he was still in bed but didn't feel as tired.

Emily visited as often as work would allow; Harold would come and pick her up when required and return her home.

Neil recovered in time for his stag night, a few nights before the wedding day. His rowdy mates got him blind drunk. They had to take him home and put him to bed, he was so inebriated.

On Neil's next visit to Emily's farm, he told her about his stag do – he was quite proud of how much he had drunk.

"It's a wonder they didn't kill you with alcohol poisoning," Emily said, disgusted at the way he had been treated.

The big day finally arrived. Emily looked radiant in her mother's lace dress. She had changed the style from calf length to a long dress. She had added lace over a satin skirt under the original dress. It worked well.

Her veil was to the floor, held by a tiara in her hair, which Jill's mother had loaned her.

For the first time Emily had her hair up. Jill had spent time backcombing her dark chestnut locks of hair and gathered them up on top of her head. Curls cascaded down from the sides and back.

Jill had also brought her makeup bag, to do a makeover on both of them. Emily looked stunningly beautiful. Her eyes sparkled; she couldn't get over how different she looked.

She wore her ring, bracelet and silver locket Neil had given her. The key was still safe inside the locket. She had bought new satin shoes and white lingerie.

Jill wore a long light blue bridesmaid dress, similar to the one she had seen in the bridal shop. Emily had made it for her. Jill also had her hair done up like Emily.

When they stepped out of the bedroom, there were gasps of amazement at how beautiful they both were. Brian was so proud of his daughter and shocked at how grown up she looked.

Brian drove her to the Parish Church in his cleaned-up car, a white sheet spread over the back seat where the Bride sat.

Neil turned his head as he stood near the altar; the wedding music was playing. He watched Emily as she approached slowly, walking with her father down the aisle. Brian lifted her veil to kiss her for the last time as an unmarried daughter.

Neil was stunned by her beauty; he hardly recognised her. She came to his side, grinning.

"You look radiant and so beautiful, just like a princess," he said admiring her.

The marriage vows were exchanged and the wedding ring placed on the bride's finger. They were finally married. They shared a loving kiss before departing in Neil's car.

The reception had been arranged at the Town Hall in Canley, where they had first met. After their meal, Brian stood up.

He toasted the newlyweds and welcomed the sixty guests. He spoke about Emily growing up and her love of animals. He told them of his admiration for her and her beauty. Emily felt so proud of him.

Neil replied on behalf of his wife, and himself and proposed a toast to the bridesmaid, Jill. She was really enjoying the attention.

Len, the best man, in return thanked Neil on behalf of the bridesmaid and told humorous stories about Neil growing up to make everyone laugh. It was a lovely occasion.

Many photographs were taken throughout the special day. Emily shone radiantly throughout, laughing and giggling – she was the happiest girl in the world.

They received a lot of presents ranging from cut glass vases to an electric Hoover vacuum cleaner.

They had a short honeymoon in Rome, Italy, Emily's first trip abroad. At that time of year, it was not too hot. They stayed at a splendid hotel, although Emily felt a little out of place as it was so regal.

They both enjoyed the sightseeing. They visited the Colosseum, and Emily shuddered at the cruelty that had once taken place there. There was the Pantheon, the Vatican and the Trevi Fountain that they also visited.

Emily's special moments were with the intimate times spent with Neil alone in their hotel room. He was a very gentle, amorous lover. Emily had never felt so much love and attention and was truly in love.

The honeymoon quickly came to an end and they travelled back to Meadows Farm, her new home.

Neil gazed at her intently as Emily came into the kitchen. They had spent their first night together in their marital home and made it very memorable.

He pressed her gently against the wall and kissed her passionately, Emily responded by curling her arms around his neck.

"It's lovely to have a wife," said Neil. Emily felt very happy and after breakfast Neil left for work.

Emily felt strange at first, in someone else's house. There was so much to learn about the electric cooker and the twin tub washing machine she wasn't used to. The routine of the house and ironing his shirts with an electric iron.

The maid, Liz, taught her everything. She was like a mother to her and they got on very well. Liz only worked part-time, two hours a day on week days.

Emily was darning socks using a wooden mushroom she had found in his mother's sewing basket. I'll have to bring my own sewing box that Neil bought me, she thought.

Neil walked in for his dinner. Emily immediately stood up and served the beef stew and dumplings she had made with baked potatoes followed by Queen's pudding, his favourite.

"That was very good," Neil remarked. "It's lovely to eat with someone. I've spent these last three years eating on my own."

Emily felt pleased with herself.

That afternoon, Neil ran into the house shouting, "Emily, get some old sheets out of the airing cupboard, we have a cow haemorrhaging after calving.

Emily rushed upstairs to gather the sheets.

"I hope she survives, poor thing." She openly prayed, handing over the sheets.

Neil came home after an exhausting day at work. Straight away Emily wanted to know if the cow had survived. Neil reassured her the cow was going to be alright.

After supper he announced he was going to a meeting. Emily was a bit surprised he was going to leave her on her own so soon.

She felt isolated and alone when he left the house. Usually she had at least one of her parents with her or her dog, Jet.

She watched the television, which was a bit of a novelty at first, and finished darning his socks. Neil arrived home after Emily had gone to bed. His breath smelt of beer.

"You've been to the pub, I can smell it," she said in dismay.

Neil smiled at her. "We always go to the pub after a meeting."

The following day Emily ventured out onto the farm. She had seen most of it on her visits before she was married. She watched the cows being milked in the byres.

The cows stood in double stalls along the wall, their necks held with a cow chain to the wall of the stall. Each cow was fed using a metal bucket in front of them. Hay racks were in easy reach, filled with hay.

The cows were milked by one of the six milking units carried to the stall and attached to the airline pipe above. The tap was turned, making the teat cups have a sucking action.

Each of the four cups were placed under the udder. The teat cups were placed one by one under the cow's washed teats, sucking onto the teat. The milk flowed into the milking unit.

Emily watched in the cooling house as the milk was poured into an open tank above the corrugated cooling machine. Tap water flowed through the machine to cool the milk as it trickled down the corrugated cooler.

The milk flowed into a churn below and was replaced by another as they filled to the rim inside. The water was caught in another churn and used to swill down the cooling house floor after milking.

Everything was washed in large wash troughs and propped up to dry on the stone slabs supported by walls.

After milking, the byres were mucked out by a shovel into a large barrow and wheeled to the walled midden outside. The heap would later be spread on the land by a tractor and muck spreader, on frosty days.

Heifers were housed loose in a fold yard. There was the calving shed that sparked memories of rolling in the straw with Neil.

The calf house had a row of pens with baby calves eager for their milk. She helped feed the calves. She put her fingers in their mouths to encourage them to suck, bending their heads down into the bucket of warm milk.

On the other side of the building were larger pens for the older calves that had been weaned off milk. They were running about, frolicking together and kicking up the straw bedding.

Emily walked down to the wood. The leaves had fallen from the trees, cushioning the ground. She could hear the stream flowing beyond the wood.

The hens were busy scratching amongst the dead leaves looking for slugs and grubs. Clucking and pecking as they walked around the wood.

She approached but they ran away. They were not like her own hens that would run towards her to be petted.

The sheep dog was chained up to its kennel; it wasn't very friendly either. The farm cats minded their own business, doing their own thing.

It made her feel a little homesick and alone. She didn't go into the beef building – she would leave that for another time.

Neil stayed in that night. He went to wash and change and then they ate supper together. Neil was tired and hadn't got much to say.

The following day Emily decided to go through all the cupboards and drawers, throughout the house, to see what she could find.

She found a family album and sat down to look at the photographs. She saw Neil growing up from a babe in arms to graduating at college. She saw Len and Ann as children, and Blaze, the Arab pony. She thought Neil was very like his father in looks.

Neil arrived for his dinner and was more talkative. Emily told him, she had found a family album and teased him about when he was younger.

Neil grinned; he liked the attention. He surprised her by saying, "I think you should learn to drive a car – when you pass your test you can have my car and I'll buy a Wolseley."

"That would be wonderful, I've always wanted to drive a car but Dad wouldn't let me." Emily was so pleased – it would mean she could go back to her farm and see her animals and see Jill.

Neil was glad she agreed. "That's settled, then, I'll give you a few lessons, but I know you will pick it up in no time, after having driven a tractor for so long."

He went out again that night, to organise something for the Young Farmers Club. She was alone again – she felt like a Queen in this mini palace but lonely and isolated from the people she knew and her beloved animals.

She wondered if she had done the right thing getting married. She wasn't required to work outside which she would have loved to have done. She felt abandoned in a way.

The following day she asked Neil, "Can Jet come and stay with me in the house? I feel so lonely here on my own when you are out."

Neil replied abruptly. "Dogs should be on a chain outside, especially working dogs like Jet."

Emily felt very down.

"Perhaps Melody could come and stay here. It would give me something to do," she begged.

Neil sighed. "We'll see," was his only reply. He was out again that night. His friends had invited him out to the pub.

Emily sat alone in the lounge feeling homesick and missing Jet terribly. She went to bed early as she felt so miserable. She never thought married life would be like this.

She thought Neil had married her and just dumped her in his house and continued his bachelor life.

The following morning at breakfast, he suggested they go out to dinner that evening. Emily was pleased. She spent time dressing for the occasion.

They drove to a large hotel outside of Townsfoot. They entered a magnificent dining room; the walls were partly panelled. The ceiling was luxuriously painted in beautiful artwork.

They wined and dined, and Emily felt very special. She asked again about Melody and Jet coming to live at Meadows Farm.

"If it makes you happy, then I will bring them for you," Neil told her. Emily was ecstatic.

The following Sunday, they both went to collect them in the Land Rover and cattle trailer. The sewing box and the rest of her belongings came too.

As usual, her parents were pleased to see them and offered them dinner. They declined as they wanted to get back. Melody was led out into the paddock to graze.

Jet was allowed in the house; he had been very excited to see Emily again. They cuddled each other. Apparently, he had slept at the bottom of her bed every night since she left.

"Now don't let it on the furniture and we will have to move the sheepskin rug out of the way," Neil said sternly.

Jet wasn't allowed in the bedroom that night. He barked incessantly and scratched at the kitchen door. He didn't like being shut away from Emily in the kitchen.

"Stupid dog, I'll never get any sleep at this rate. Fetch him up, so I can get some sleep."

Emily bought Jet upstairs; he lay quietly and content at the bottom of Emily's side of the bed.

Neil wasn't very pleased with this arrangement and wished he had never agreed for the dog to be allowed in the house. But Emily was very happy she had Jet as a companion and to comfort her now.

Emily invited her parents for Sunday dinner with Neil's permission. She prepared the dining room for the meal. She found the best cutlery and crockery in the dresser.

She laid out the place mats. She rolled the serviettes into their silver serviette rings she had found. She placed the cut glass wine glasses onto silver coasters, on the table and arranged a table decoration.

Her parents arrived later. Brian was very talkative with Neil and they went into the lounge to discuss the weather and farming. Margaret stayed with Emily to help finish off cooking the roast beef, vegetables and roast potatoes.

Her mother had peeped into the dining room; she expressed to Emily how well she had arranged the table. She was surprised how lovely the house was – this was her first visit.

Emily had made an apple pie using the stored apples out of the orchard. She made some custard using milk from the cows. They all enjoyed their hearty meal.

Neil showed Brian outside, while Emily showed her mother upstairs. Margaret was very impressed by it all and was, secretly, very envious of everything Emily had.

They all came together in the lounge. The open fire was ablaze and crackled in the grate. Jet was lying on his new rug in front of the fire, very content.

Neil and Emily had enjoyed her parents coming for dinner. Neil wished his parents had been there too.

Neil came in the following day for breakfast in a terrible mood. Emily had never seen him like this and was a little afraid of him.

"What is wrong?" she asked quietly. Neil grunted and sat down.

"The tractor wouldn't start this morning, the tractor man is on holiday, so he couldn't fix it," he moaned. They ate their breakfast in silence.

Neil carried on his bachelor's lifestyle. Emily appeared to be well down the list of his priorities. It was not what she had expected of married life at all.

She tried to mention it to her parents but they had no sympathy. "You've made your bed, now lie in it," they told her. She wasn't to come back home to live. Her mother couldn't believe she was so ungrateful with so much that had landed in her lap with no effort.

Emily and Neil were invited to one of Neil's friend's parties. When there was a lull in the conversation, the host would pick on Emily.

"You're quiet, what have you got to say for yourself?"

The shy Emily flushed; she was tongue-tied.

Anything she did say, the host turned it into something sexual, making Emily blush deeper.

They all laughed at her including her new husband. She felt his friends were very arrogant and rude.

She expected Neil to stand up for her, but he appeared to be joining his friends. She hated the evening, she felt ridiculed and humiliated and wanted to go home.

To take her mind off it, the following day, she started preparing for Christmas. Baking a Christmas cake and a large Christmas pudding, she thought she would invite her parents on Christmas Day. It did brighten up her day, she loved Christmas.

She was writing letters to Jill whenever she could, although she didn't mention that the marriage was nothing like she had thought it would be. Jill would probably only repeat what her parents had said.

Emily was able to spend time with Melody and Jet. Melody was wintering out in the paddock – she had a stone shed as a shelter from the wind and rain.

She would make sure she had enough hay every day and her water trough was clean and full. She would occasionally pick Melody's hooves up one by one and scrape them out with a hoof pick to check her feet.

She was thankful her animals were here. They were her best friends and she loved them dearly.

A SURPRISE

Emily wasn't feeling well, by mid-December. She was preparing meat for a stew and she felt squeamish. The following morning, she vomited in the bathroom and had a pain in her lower abdomen.

She caught the bus at the farm lane end and went to see the doctor in Finley. She had missed two periods but thought it was the change in her life. Her mother was the same after she married.

The Doctor examined her and smiled.

"Congratulations, my dear, you are pregnant."

Emily didn't know whether to laugh or cry with the pain of the abdominal cramps.

Neil was over the moon when Emily announced it to him that evening. He kissed her gently and said she mustn't work too hard to give the baby every chance.

The following day, Neil surprised her. He had gone into town and bought a beautiful diamond necklace for her.

Emily's eyes sparkled at the attention she was receiving from him now. He couldn't love her enough. She hoped the baby would be a boy, a son and heir, for him.

Once the cramps subsided Emily started looking forward to having her first child. She eagerly started knitting little jackets, bonnets and booties in neutral colours.

Her parents were wild with joy to hear their wonderful news, their first grandchild on the way. Brian said he would make a cot for the baby. Margaret would make some soft toys and a matinee coat.

The Christmas dinner was extra special with toasts to the unborn child. Everyone was happy including Emily. Neil had given her a large leather jewellery box as a present. When she opened it, there were a pair of diamond earrings to match her necklace.

That evening Emily had a few painful cramps and miscarried; it just all came away at once while she was in the bathroom. She was in shock. She sat on the bathroom floor and cried. How can this happen to me, she cried – she wanted this baby so badly.

Neil was hammering at the locked bathroom door.

"Are you alright in there? What's wrong?"

Emily slowly unlocked the door and opened it.

"We have lost our baby; I've had a miscarriage." She flung her arms around him and sobbed.

Neil kissed her forehead and tried to comfort her.

"You're young enough to have plenty of babies, don't worry, we can try again."

Emily felt miserable for weeks; no one, not even Jet, could alter this gloom that had descended over her.

Neil tried his best to be more loving and attentive towards her. He took her out for a meal and to the theatre on her birthday to try and cheer her up. He showered her with gifts.

The maid had been a comfort to her – she had experienced a miscarriage and knew what Emily was going through. Later that year the maid had to hand in her notice. She needed the time to look after her mother who was seriously ill.

Emily would miss her terribly. It was her company she enjoyed. They would laugh and joke as they worked together. The time seemed to just fly by.

Neil was still going out regularly on his own. Emily was alone in bed one night. Jet was curled up asleep at the bottom of her bed.

Suddenly he jumped off the bed barking and growling aggressively. He ran to the window, jumping up and putting his paws on the window sill, barking crazily.

Emily thought there was someone prowling around outside. She was very afraid; she was not in screaming distance of anyone. She thought she would be safe just staying still.

Jet started running around the room barking and growling like a mad dog. His hackles were raised and he was baring his teeth and snarling. He was foaming at the mouth. She began to wonder if he was rabid. She had never seen him like this.

After a while he stopped barking and just paced the room excitedly. Finally, he jumped on the bed and fell asleep. Emily didn't know what to think, she had heard nothing.

When Neil came into the bedroom later, she told him all about what had happened. He hadn't got an answer for her but was glad she was safe.

At breakfast time, Neil told her a cow had got out during the night. There were hoof indentations on the lawn in front of the house. Emily was relieved and so pleased that Jet was trying to protect her.

Finally, spring arrived, her favourite time of the year, which lightened her mood. She had passed her driving test and Neil had given her his Hillman Minx. She now felt free to visit her parents and Jill whenever she liked.

Jet loved to sit in the passenger seat and look out of the windscreen. He was her constant companion.

Emily helped at lambing, Neil only had about 30 ewes, used as a foraging flock on the arable land. Twins were born to one ewe, a large gimmer lamb, and a runt – it was a tup.

Neil told Frank, the stockman, to 'Knock the runt on its head', its mother had abandoned it. But Emily picked the poor thing up and zipped it up inside her anorak to keep it warm. She wasn't going to allow them to kill it.

She haltered the ewe and tied it to its pen. She milked one teat, while the other twin lamb sucked the other teat.

Emily gave the runt the milk from a feeding bottle. She called him Spot, after the black spot near its tail. She took it to the warm kitchen and put it in a large box.

Jet immediately climbed in the box and licked the lamb. Both lay down and snuggled up to each other and fell asleep.

Emily thought how marvellous the animal kingdom is to care for each other, even different species. Jet instinctively knew the little tup needed help.

Emily had penned up the gimmer lamb so it didn't go with all the milk from its mother. She was going every four hours to milk the ewe, at the same time allowing the gimmer to suck. This helped let down the ewe's milk, in order to milk her. Spot eventually grew stronger.

There was another ewe that had a very difficult birth. The first lamb was coming shoulder first. Emily pushed it back and turned it – it was useful having long slender hands for this job.

She managed to get the head and two front feet coming forward; it was soon born with a pull. It was struggling to breathe so she cleared its mouth and nose and hung it up by its back legs in her right hand to drain its lungs.

The lamb coughed and spluttered. It shook its head making its little ears flap. It was going to survive, she thought, and she laid it in front of the ewe for her to lick it clean and bond with it.

Her second lamb was coming, back feet first, so she helped it on its way. The last triplet was the largest – fortunately it was coming the right way and Emily gently pulled it out with the help of the mother's contractions.

The largest lamb was taken off the ewe as the ewe only had two teats. Emily called the lamb Molly.

Emily went out late that night to see that everything was alright with the ewe. She had had a bad time giving birth. The ewe was in a pen with two of her lambs. Molly was with Spot in the kitchen.

One lamb was arching its back with cold; it was wet, it must have stood behind the ewe when she urinated. The other was trying to suck but not getting any milk from her teat. The ewe looked very miserable.

Emily penned up the lambs to give the ewe a rest from them. She dried the wet lamb with straw. She brought in some fresh hay, feed and water for the ewe and scattered some clean straw down for bedding, to make her feel comfortable.

The ewe lay down exhausted and ate the food put in front of her. Emily bottle fed her lambs. When their tummies were full, they lay down and fell asleep.

Emily slipped out in the early hours, to make sure they were alright. The ewe looked brighter and was contentedly chewing her cud. The lambs were still fast asleep.

At six o'clock Emily got up and entered the pen. The lambs woke up and bleated for their mother. Emily released the lambs out of their pen and they ran to the ewe.

The ewe stood up and Emily could see that her udder was full. The lambs each sucked on a teat till they were full. Emily felt pleased: there could have been two dead lambs if she had not helped them.

Molly, the other lamb, had been fed on her mother's milk for a couple of feeds and joined Spot on powdered milk, mixed with water and then warmed.

Molly was returned to her mother the next day. Once the ewe realised Molly smelt different with the other milk, she wouldn't let her suck from her.

So, there was more milk for the other two. Molly was still being bottle fed. Her mother allowed her to be with her and to walk around the field with her family when they were outside permanently.

Emily would stand at the gate and shout "lamb-ee, lamb-ee". To her delight, Spot and Molly would appear scampering up the field. They would eagerly feed on the two bottles she had prepared, standing side by side, wagging their tails. It made Emily smile.

Molly, Spot and the other two lambs would trail around after the ewe grazing – she looked as if she had had all four of them herself.

Emily helped Frank castrate the rest of the baby tups and tail all the lambs. Some of the lambs were beginning to run around in groups, skipping and jumping as they played. She loved lambing time and had forgotten all about her miscarriage.

At breakfast the following morning Neil arrived.

"That damned cow," shouted Neil as he slammed the kitchen door.

"What's the matter now?" Emily questioned.

Neil told her a cow in the perimeter field, had broken all the fences back to the farm during the night, to get back to her calf in the calf house. He was very angry as this had happened for two nights in a row.

He had to go and mend all the fences again. It was a job he didn't need as they were very busy that day. Greg the cow man was on holiday, so he was short staffed.

Emily tried to explain. "She is trying to get back to her baby. Cows have emotions too, you know. I would do the same thing if someone took my baby away from me."

"Don't talk rubbish, animals do not have emotions." With that he pushed Emily violently away. She was put off balance and fell backwards, banging her head on the wall and she blacked out.

When she came around, Neil was stood over her shouting, "Get up, get up." He was afraid he had killed her like Joe Stokes. Emily stood up dazed.

"Are you alright?" he asked. Emily nodded.

Neil was still in shock at what he could have done. He stormed out and slammed the door behind him. He hadn't known how to cope with his awful memories.

Emily was shocked to the core; he hadn't even hugged her or kissed her. He had only shown his cold, ruthless side she had never seen before. Nothing more was said about it.

That night when she went to bed, there was a little parcel on her side of the bed. She opened it; it was a little ornament of a border collie sheepdog, just like Jet.

Her heart melted; Neil did care after all. That night Neil made love to her in his gentle, amorous way – all was forgiven.

Neil was still going out a lot at nights. They were leading separate lives most of the time as she hardly saw him. He worked long hours on the farm. They rarely went out as a couple.

In July Emily went to visit Melody in her paddock. She instantly knew something was wrong. Melody was lying flat out on the grass.

She ran over to her and knelt beside her.

"Melody, Melody my beautiful pony, please don't die."

Melody's ears twitched but she was not responding otherwise. Emily stroked her pony, tears rolled down her cheeks and fell onto Melody's neck.

Melody drew her last breath and her nostrils quivered, then nothing. She had slipped away peacefully. Emily lay her head on Melody's neck and sobbed.

Neil heard her sobs as he walked out of the yard. He came running towards her. He stood over her and looked at the dead animal.

"It had to happen one day," he said. "She was a very old pony. Come, Emily, I'll take you to the house. I'll arrange the Knacker man to come for a dead calf and the pony this morning."

Emily didn't watch the Knacker man winch the corpse into his wagon and drive away. She couldn't bear to see the undignified operation to her beloved Melody. Neil saw to it all instead.

Emily felt an emptiness inside, part of her had died with Melody that day. She remembered how she had grown up with this gentle animal. The wonderful times they had had together.

Jet sensed she was miserable and tried to nuzzle his nose under her hand on the arm of the chair. Emily responded and stroked his head and back. It was calming for her.

It was never the same without Melody; her paddock stood empty. There were no more trips to see her and feed her ever again.

A new travelling salesman visited that summer. He knocked on the door while Neil and Emily were having tea.

"Come on in, we were just having a bite to eat before milking. Would you like some tea?" Emily asked in her friendly way.

He agreed and introduced himself to them as Ken. He had come to sell household goods if Emily was interested. Neil got up to go.

"I'll leave you to it, I'm off to do the milking."

Ken began laying out his wares on the kitchen table for Emily to inspect.

"I'll have some clothes pegs and a few tea towels please," she told him handing him some cash out of her purse.

Ken gathered the rest of the items into his bag, chatting away about his life and how he became a salesman for a company. He told her he was now self-employed and doing very well. He hoped to expand into larger items like Hoover vacuum cleaners.

He was a cheerful kind of man. Tall and slim, with dark hair. Emily clicked with him immediately, he was so easy going. They talked for a while, before Emily realised the time and had to get on and prepare the supper.

She waved at him as he climbed into his green Morris Mini van. She bumped into him in Townsfoot about a week later. She had popped into a cafe for a drink and there he was sat alone.

Ken immediately recognised her and offered her a seat on the same table as him. He ordered her a cup of tea and a cake. They chatted about life and then he had to leave.

Neil found out at the pub that night – a farmer told Neil that his wife had seen Ken and Emily in the cafe together. Neil was not very pleased.

The following day at breakfast he approached Emily with the subject. She didn't deny it. As far as she was concerned it was totally innocent. She continued making the breakfast.

Neil had been building up a jealous rage inside him for some time. It had grown stronger until he was out of control. He began shouting at Emily.

"Don't ever let me hear you ever talking to a man again when I'm not there, do you hear me." He got up from his seat at the table and stood menacingly behind her. She turned.

She could see his eyes had changed; they had madness glaring out of them at her.

"Don't worry, there was absolutely nothing in it," Emily told him in a quiet voice to try and calm the situation.

"If you ever leave me, I'll make sure you end up in the gutter, do you understand?"

Emily turned away to attend to placing the bacon on his plate.

"Don't you turn away from me when I'm talking to you," Neil snarled. He then grabbed her by the arm and flung her across the room.

Emily was taken by surprise, she hit her head on the skirting board ridge, and blacked out. Neil was frantic, he had done it again and this time it took longer for her to come around.

Emily was very dazed and was not talking properly. Neil carried her to the bedroom and gently laid her on the bed.

"You are a little concussed, try to sleep. You will be better soon."

Jet was licking her hand when she woke up. She gave him a big hug. She needed a loving hug – she was still shocked at what had happened. It was all surreal to her, she couldn't believe Neil was capable of this behaviour.

The incident was never mentioned by either of them. Emily didn't want to get him in a rage, for fear of being hurt again.

The following day, she found a parcel on the side of the bed. She opened it carefully. It was another ornament, this time of a black Fell Pony. It was just like Melody. Tears welled up in her eyes and an emotional lump formed in her throat.

She broke down emotionally and cried. She cried for the loss of Melody and cried for the loss of her loving marriage. Jet was there to comfort her the best he could. He didn't like her to be distressed.

Emily carried on being the dutiful wife. Although her heart was disintegrating bit by bit, she was just going through the motions of married life, hoping that things would get better.

Ken called in at the farm a month later. Neil was at the auction in Townsfoot for the day so Emily thought it would be safe to allow him in for a mug of tea.

"You've lost your sparkle, Emily, are you ill?" Ken asked, rather worried for her.

Emily blurted out her marriage was going downhill and she wasn't allowed to speak to men anymore. She then burst into tears. She couldn't help it.

All the emotions of the last year had been building and building. Now the great dam wall holding it all together had suddenly collapsed.

Ken was shocked and put his arm around her to try to comfort her. Emily felt the warm caring arm enveloping her and wished so much to be loved.

Ken said he would come again but if Neil was on the farm he would stay outside. He wanted to make sure she was alright.

Neil had remained at the auction and then gone to the pub with his mates so he was late back. At least it had given Emily time to compose herself.

Life carried on. Emily helped with hay making and harvest which took her mind off things. She was at least working with Neil and saw a lot of him. He appeared to have settled down; there were no more terrifying rages.

They continued to try for a baby but whether it was the emotional stress or not, nothing happened. Love making was never the same for Emily after his violence. She saw him in a different light.

Emily was helping with milking that winter. Greg the cow man and Frank the stockman, they were off work with the flu for about a week.

She enjoyed working with the cows and they soon got to know her and trust her. She would sing softly to them as she cupped on the teat cups.

She noticed one particular cow seemed to be pretending to eat. It was very peculiar.

"Hey, Neil, come and look at this," Emily called out to Neil at the end of the byre. Neil stood back to observe the cow.

"It's got wooden tongue, it can't eat properly," Neil said, surprised that Emily had noticed. He felt its tongue – it was swollen, which confirmed what he had thought.

"I'll ring the vet, it just needs antibiotics and it will be fine," Neil added.

Emily prepared the buckets for the calves, pouring the cows' milk into a couple.

She carried the buckets into the calf house. The calves were already on their feet waiting for a feed. She placed them in the metal rings at the front of their pens.

These older calves knew what to do and immediately poked their heads through the space in the bars. Their heads quickly lowered into the bucket to drink the milk, their little tails wagging and their legs dancing with excitement.

Neil brought in more buckets of warm milk. Emily climbed into another pen. The little black calf had heard it was feeding time and ran excitedly, head first, into the wall at the back.

It was strange behaviour, but they had realised it was blind. It was obviously hearing the noise bounce off the back wall, so that's where it ran to.

It had been a premature birth. The vet had reassured them that it would get its sight back eventually. Emily used her fingers to encourage it to suck, before lowering its head into the bucket. Her heart poured out to this particular baby calf.

Neil and Emily came in exhausted that night. They didn't bother to wash and change for supper – it was too late. Emily dished out some homemade chicken and vegetable soup with bread rolls. Followed by apple crumble and cream.

They were glad when the men recovered from flu and returned to work and everything got back to normal.

Emily visited her parents before Christmas to invite them over for Christmas Day as usual. Her parents had had mains electricity, installed by an overhead cable.

Her mother proudly showed her the twin tub she had bought and the electric oven with an overhead grill, although she still preferred the range. Life was a little easier working in the house for her now.

Her father was pleased to see Emily; he had recently had a pint in The Bull with Neil so he had been updated about the news of their farm. He showed off his new electric tools in the workshop.

The following day Emily met Jill in Canley, at their usual cafe. Jill was in her second year at teacher training college. She was studying to be a primary school teacher – she wanted to teach in a village school once she was qualified.

Emily had written to her about the sad loss of Melody. Jill didn't quite understand, not being an animal lover herself. They appeared to be so different.

They had taken two very different paths in life and hadn't really got much in common, apart from their school days together. Jill had stayed on to do 'O' and 'A' Levels before college.

Emily hadn't kept in touch with her other friends at school so didn't have many friends of her own. Only people she had met casually in Finley and Townsfoot.

Christmas Day had arrived. Emily prepared a splendid table and meal, but her heart was not really in the celebrations. Her memory was going back to the previous year when she had lost the baby.

Everyone else was merry. Neil had bought her some sexy lingerie and a red dress which she wore for the occasion. She looked stunning.

Neil was taking secret glances when he could – he still admired her beauty. He made love to her again that night. Emily pretended to enjoy it but wished he would leave her alone.

He never sensed her sadness; he didn't feel any empathy. When he was satisfied, he rolled over to his side of the bed and quickly fell asleep.

It took a while for Emily to fall asleep; thoughts in her head would not leave. She so desperately wanted a better marriage. She felt so lonely and used.

She hardly saw Neil most days. She wasn't paid for any work she did outside. It was still Neil's business; she had not been made a partner. Neil had told her she had full board and lodgings and Jet's keep. Holidays and clothes were paid for – what more did she need?

She told him she wanted to have a little money of her own to invest. Neil had replied, "What's mine is yours, only it's in my name." He would grin, he liked having that control over her.

New Year celebrations was a time Emily dreaded. They were usually invited to the house of one of Neil's friends. She was always made the source of ridicule and felt very humiliated. It got worse as they drank more.

1971 was no different. The host from a previous party was there, embarrassing her and making her blush. She hated it.

It amused everyone including Neil. He would get very drunk and do silly things with other wives; like getting locked in a cupboard with them or rolling around on the floor with them. Much to Emily's disgust.

EMILY DISAPPEARS

On the morning of Emily's birthday, Neil was in the kitchen finishing his breakfast.

"Think about where you would like to go this evening for your birthday meal," Neil said, in a jovial mood.

When he left, Emily sat down and looked at her latest gift, a sewing machine. She was thrilled with it and wanted to start sewing up a new dress, made out of some pretty material ready for the evening.

She really wanted to go to a small restaurant in Canley – it was under new management and had been completely refurbished. She had been there when she was younger with her parents.

She got herself ready that evening. She was excited to wear her new dress – she was very pleased with how it had turned out. She swung around in it, admiring her work in front of the mirror.

Neil came into the kitchen in a bad mood that evening. He didn't like what she was wearing.

"You're not wearing that. Go put on your red dress, I gave you."

Emily's felt destroyed and didn't bother to antagonise him, by saying, no.

She put on the red dress in the bedroom. Neil entered and smiled.

"I like you in that dress, it suits you." He undressed ready for a shower.

"Did you think about where we should go?" asked Neil.

"Yes, The Green Man at Canley," Emily began excitedly, "it's been refurbished and–"

Neil interrupted her as he put on his dressing gown. "No, we are not going there. I'll take you to that place in Townsfoot, The Arms Hotel, it will be better there."

Emily felt totally depleted of the excitement she had built up during the day. She said nothing.

They did have a lovely meal at the Arms Hotel – Neil's bad mood had disappeared and he was quite cheerful and chatty.

Friends of Neil arrived at the bar so when he went to get another beer, he stayed to talk, longer than he intended.

Emily was furious at being left alone at the table. It was her birthday, after all. She felt her evening had been totally ruined. If they had gone to Canley none of his friends would have been there.

There was a storm in February. The roof of the calving shed blew off. It was an old corrugated iron roof.

Emily saw the whole thing from the landing window of the house.

Each sheet was ripped off one by one and flew in the air like kites. One by one they glided down onto the grass in the field.

She remembered there was a cow in the shed with its newly born calf. She ran outside, putting on her anorak. She looked over the half door. The wind was swirling around like a whirlwind, whipping up the straw inside.

The cow was stood motionless with its eyes closed to stop the dust and straw getting into her eyes. The calf appeared to be asleep.

Emily shouted to the men but the roar of the wind deafened her cries. The rain pelted her face as she ran, bending her body into the wind to find them.

The men came to rescue the cow and calf and drove them into another building. The cow was taken away to join the milk herd. The calf was penned up on some dry straw.

Lambing season went well that year, Emily's favourite time. There was just one old ewe that had to be taken to slaughter. She had one lamb but her uterus was so dry and paper thin the lamb had ruptured it during lambing.

Emily felt so sad as Neil drove the ewe away. The ewe was calling out to her new born and the little lamb was bleating back to her – it was heart breaking.

Emily hand reared the lamb with a feeding bottle and named her Lotty. Jet helped with mothering it. The little lamb grew up thinking it was a dog and would go everywhere with Jet on his travels around the yard.

Lotty joined the flock to eventually have lambs of her own, like Molly had. Spot had been sold at the auction.

The men were getting ready for haymaking. Greasing the machinery and repairing any damage. Neil came in for dinner in a bad mood. Dinner was eaten in silence.

Emily couldn't even remember how the conversation started as Neil stood up to go back to work.

It eventually led onto the fact that Emily hardly saw him since he had started the foundations for the new cowshed. He became enraged.

"You are such an ungrateful cow," Neil shouted. "I give you everything. Women would give their right arms to marry me."

He shoved her violently up against the wall.

"Your parents won't have you back, your dad told me that. Any stories you tell about me, they won't believe you. They think so highly of me; they treat me like an only son. You're nothing," he said screaming at her.

His hands grabbed her neck and he squeezed until she nearly passed out. Jet was barking and snarling at him in a frenzy. Neil flung her away and stormed out. Jet had probably saved her life.

Emily landed on all fours, desperately trying to get her breath back. She then held her swollen neck with her shaking right hand.

Jet ran around her and began to lovingly lick her face. She hugged him desperately as if he was the only loving soul on Earth, which to her he was. She cried uncontrollably; Jet licked the tears away but couldn't mend her shattered heart.

She was so distraught and depleted of energy, that she couldn't lift herself up. She thought about suicide but could not leave her dearest companion, Jet, behind. What could she do, where could she go? she thought. She didn't have any money of her own or even a bank account.

She decided to make the best of things here and try not to antagonise Neil. She carried on being the dutiful wife in a robotic kind of way. But inside she was dreadfully unhappy. Only Jet gave her the motivation to live.

She helped at hay making; it was very hard work but she enjoyed it. It took her back to her childhood days working in the meadow with her father and uncle, her rolling in the bales and her mother driving the tractor.

That's all she had now, memories, nothing really to look forward to in life anymore. She no longer wanted Neil's child.

Harvest time came and went, the year was flying by. The crops were average but would see them through the winter, if it wasn't a severe one.

Emily developed a spot on the end of her nose; it was very embarrassing for her. Of course, Neil noticed straight away, he reminded her of it every time he saw her.

He appeared to enjoy pointing it out to her, making her feel even more self-conscious about it. He told her she looked ugly with it, which lowered Emily's self-esteem and confidence. He had become very narcissistic during their short marriage.

Neil had arrived home from the auction one day and saw a pool of blood near the back door. He thought it was Emily's blood. He wondered if she had been attacked or she had been wounded by an accident.

He ran into the house calling her name, but there was no reply. He ran upstairs but there was no sign of her.

He rushed around to where the men were working and told them about the blood he had seen. They told him it belonged to his sheepdog. Emily had taken him to the vet's.

Apparently, Neil's sheepdog had returned home after a fight with another dog and came to the back door. Emily heard him whining. When she saw the fountain of blood spurting out from his snout, she rushed to get some pads and tape.

Neil was at the auction so she drove the dog, in her own car, to the vet's. The vet had to give it a general anaesthetic as it was a bit aggressive with him.

He found the torn vein and tied both the ends. He then stitched the gash in the snout. The dog was heavy to carry back to her car. It had not come around from the anaesthetic and it felt like a dead weight.

Once home, she laid it on his bed of straw in the kennel. She remembered to chain him up and made sure he had plenty of clean water in his bowl.

"Thanks for taking the dog to the vet's," Neil said later.

"I didn't want him to be suffering so I took him immediately. He will be alright now once he comes out of the general anaesthetic," Emily replied.

Neil was in a bad mood again at supper. Emily had learnt not to say anything. Neil was waiting for her to ask what was wrong but she didn't ask. So, he thought he would tell her.

"A heifer calved a few weeks ago but it doesn't appear to be giving any milk," he told her.

"What's wrong with it?" Emily asked curiously.

"No idea," was Neil's abrupt reply.

The following afternoon, Emily went to observe the cows to see if one of the other cows was suckling from it.

There was a slight raise in the field, and there she saw this young cow laid down on her side using the slight raise to assist her to bend right over and suckle from her own teats!

She had never seen anything like it and wouldn't have believed anyone who had told her, without seeing it from her own eyes.

Neil was a little doubtful himself when he heard. The men put a collar of blunt spikes on the young cow's neck which stopped her suckling herself again.

Ken, the salesman, visited a few times, but he always stayed in the yard. He didn't want to cause any more trouble for Emily. He looked forward to seeing her; he thought she was a lovely young woman.

Emily always smiled at him and made him welcome. She usually bought something from him and had a little chat if Neil was not in the yard. Ken told her his business was doing very well. Emily mentioned nothing about Ken to Neil to prevent any arguments.

12th October was Neil and Emily's wedding anniversary. They decided to go away for a weekend to the Lake District staying at Sharron House Hotel. It was set in beautiful manicured gardens, with a lovely terrace and fantastic views.

They had lovely meals, duck, pheasant, quail's eggs and an array of delicious desserts.

They lived like royalty. They toured around the Lake District in Neil's Wolseley car. There were breath-taking views in the October sunshine.

Neil was no longer an amorous lover. He had become aggressive; it was more lust than love. There were no more romantic words to woo her, instead she was called a whore!

She hated this aggressive style of sex and was a little afraid. Neil was relentless, he was ravaging her like an animal at every opportunity.

She wanted to get back home to Jet and a normal life. Neil had enjoyed this exciting new game of lovemaking, he felt empowered and exhilarated by it.

Jet was pleased to see Emily when she arrived home. The men told her Jet had lain near the farm gate every day, waiting for her return. At night Frank had fed him and taken him back to the house.

While Emily was out shopping in Townsfoot, a friend she had made there, joined her for a cup of tea in the cafe.

"Your husband loves the attention of the ladies after the committee meetings at the pub," she told her. Emily didn't look pleased.

"He stands there, pint in hand, with about six women all stood round him. They are all chatting and laughing together. He looks as if he is enjoying himself."

Emily had not told her that her marriage was a wreck, she just murmured that he loved attention.

A large cattle wagon came into the yard at the farm, to collect the beef cattle to sell at the auction. Emily went to help drive and load the cattle. Jet was walking around the yard observing the action.

When the cattle were loaded, the men and Emily had a mug of tea with the driver, to let the cattle settle. While they were in the kitchen, they heard a loud piercing scream from Jet. They all raced out into the yard to find a horrific sight.

The front wagon wheel had run over Jet. He was still under the wheel, dead. Emily screamed. Neil forced her back into the house; she was near to collapse.

She cried relentlessly; she felt her heart had been ripped out of her. She would never see or feel Jet again, never have her tears licked away or be hugged by his soft warm body.

The men removed Jet from under the wheel. Frank buried Jet's broken body in the orchard and marked his grave with a wooden cross. The wagon driver confessed he had not pulled his handbrake on fully.

Emily felt very alone now, there were no friends left, she was devastated in her grief. She had no appetite to eat or the enthusiasm to do her work.

She visited Jet's grave every day and sometimes placed some wildflowers there, just to show him she would always remember him.

Neil had been patient for a while with Emily but now he wanted his sex life back. Emily couldn't cope and turned away. Neil felt very frustrated but left her alone.

Emily had been sound asleep and suddenly woke up one night. It was pitch black; she didn't know who was attacking her. A man had grabbed her and pulled her violently across the bed.

She thought someone had broken into the house and had murdered her husband. She thought he was on the floor in a pool of blood and the intruder was going to kill her.

She was frozen with terror. She couldn't move a muscle or even scream. She was crazily being thrown around the bed. Then her body was violated. She wished Jet had been there to save her.

Her eyes were becoming more accustomed to the dark and she could see that it was Neil who was the attacker and rapist. She came out of her frozen state, slightly relieved it was the devil she knew rather than the devil she didn't know.

She was very confused. *Why is he doing this to me,* she thought. She told him to stop hurting her but he carried on more ruthlessly.

She was badly bruised and sore, the pain amplified due to the extreme distress she was in. He left her to go and milk the cows. She felt exhausted and collapsed into a sleep.

She didn't go downstairs to make the breakfast; she could not face the world after her ordeal. She felt traumatised and utterly miserable and degraded.

Neil came upstairs to see her. She told him she thought an intruder had done that to her and he had already been murdered. He bent over her and kissed her gently on the forehead and said, "sorry," in a soft voice.

Neil had enjoyed the experience, it was just a bit of rough and tumble for him, he didn't realise the horror she had gone through. Later that morning Emily had to go to Townsfoot. She didn't want to go out – she had not recovered from her horrifying experience.

Her car was not in the lean-to. So, she walked up the yard to find it. Neil was attending to it.

"I need my car, I have to go and pick up my groceries," she explained.

"I've started changing the oil, and I'm checking other things too, so if you have to go now, use the bus," Neil said abruptly.

Emily thought she would leave his dinner ready on the table, ham sandwiches and fruit cake and catch the 11 am bus.

She was walking across the bridge in Townsfoot when she stopped and peered over the bridge wall. Below she could see the clear water as it ran over the stones and boulders.

She thought the water was a bit like life, in a way, starting off as a stream with not much to hinder it. Then it flowed into a larger river with more obstacles to negotiate.

It would eventually flow into the sea where its world was a huge place. There were massive sea creatures, pollution, hurricanes and ships to disturb the calm surface water. Then the water would evaporate and condense into clouds.

In a way like people dying, she thought. Perhaps we do come back, reincarnate like the clouds shed rain back to earth. To start the whole process again but in a different stream or life.

The sun shone on the ripples making them shine. It reminded her about her sterling silver locket she always wore. She lifted it out from under her blouse. She opened it carefully to retrieve the little key inside.

The same key that Jill and her had joked about. The key that would open Neil's heart. She hated that key now and threw it into the river below. She believed she had opened the heart of a monster and did not know how to escape from him.

She completed her shopping in a daze. Too many traumatic things had happened recently and she could not comprehend everything fully.

She was struggling to carry her shopping bags, when a kind and familiar voice behind her said, "I'll help you with those – where is your car?"

It was Ken, the salesman.

"I couldn't bring my car, Neil was working on it," Emily replied.

He could see she looked upset and insisted on taking her to her farm road end in his van.

As they walked towards his van, she noticed it was a completely different one. It was a blue Commer van and Emily commented on it.

"It's a lot different from your Morris Mini."

"Yes, I needed a bigger van now, I'm selling larger stuff," he said, grinning.

They sat in his van and chatted. Emily broke down when she told him about the sad news of Jet. He put his hand on hers and tried to comfort her.

Neil had to make his own tea at 4 o'clock. Emily would be just getting on the bus from Townsfoot, he thought. He would be milking by the time she arrived home.

Neil arrived home from milking at 6 o'clock ready for his supper. He shouted for Emily as there was no meal ready. There was no reply.

He ran upstairs and searched all the bedrooms and bathroom: no sign of her. He searched the lounge and dining room; everything was deadly silent.

He grabbed some baking from the cake tin and jumped into his car. He ate it, while driving to Townsfoot – he was determined to try and find her. Nearly all the shops had closed for the day and it was dark and getting very cold.

He drove around the streets searching for her. Occasionally he would stop and ask if anyone had seen her. Everyone shook their heads and walked on.

He even drove to the hospital to inquire there. No one had seen her. He began to wonder if she had taken off with Ken.

The thought of his wife in another man's arms threw him into a frenzied rage. *How dare she run off,* he thought. *I'll kill that man.* He drove wildly back home to see if she had come home.

He was thinking of all the things he would do to her and tell her, when he would get home. He was in a foul temper.

He frantically searched the rooms again, in a complete rage. The house gave up nothing, only silence and loneliness, not even Jet to greet him.

He sat on a chair at the kitchen table, his head in his hands and he cried for the first time in many years. He was a broken man.

She had finally deserted him and he was now alone, he thought. He knew he couldn't live without her; he needed a wife to look after him. He found a bottle of whiskey in the lounge and began to drink excessively. His life had completely fallen apart.

He had a large hangover the next day. Greg, the cowman had carried on without him. Neil eventually surfaced and later told the men that Emily had left him and run off with Ken. Neil couldn't see any other explanation.

If he had known where Ken lived, he would have gone over to his house and shot him, he was that angry at having his wife snatched from him.

Neil drove up to Browtop Farm to see Brian and Margaret, her parents. They were pleased to see him and invited him in. They could see he wasn't his usual self and let him explain what was wrong in his own good time.

Neil talked about farming and the weather, trying to avoid telling them what he had really come for. Margaret brought in tea and homemade cakes for them.

"How is Emily coping now after Jet was killed?" Margaret inquired. There was a long silence.

Margaret was concerned. Neil bent over and put his head in his hands.

"She has run off," he replied angrily and upset.

"Who with?" Brian demanded to know. "I'll kill the bastard."

Neil told them she had been making eyes at Ken the salesman, they had been seen together in the cafe in Townsfoot some time ago. He had no idea where he lived.

"He probably doesn't even live around here," Margaret said angrily. "I'll ask around and see if I can get his address. We want her back; she is your wife and our daughter."

Neil went home to his dark, silent house. There was no cheering open fire to sit by, no wife to bring him a hot mug of cocoa. He felt gutted. He was going from rage to self-pity, alternately in his head.

He was usually in full control of situations but not this time. He didn't know what was going on and hated that.

He hated Emily for landing him in this mess. He knew people would talk.

He made up his mind to forget her, he could never, ever forgive her for this. It was the only way he would cope with it all. How dare she embarrass him like this, he raged.

Word quickly spread throughout Finley, Townsfoot and Canley. Some people were shocked that Emily could have even thought about leaving him.

Some thought Neil had treated her badly enough for her to leave, others thought he had killed her in one of his rages.

Life carried on as normal at the farm; Neil employed a mature housekeeper part-time, to shop, cook, bake, wash and clean the house. He wasn't going to do any 'woman's work' as he used to call it.

He went out every night. He couldn't stand the loneliness at home. He started flirting with women, particularly a single woman named Janet Bennett.

She was taller than Emily and more outgoing. She was slim with dark brown hair. She was a veterinary nurse at his local vet's in Townsfoot. She was about six years younger than Neil.

Neil felt the same excitement about her as he had meeting Emily. He knew he had to be cautious. Emily might still turn up and they were still officially married.

Without knowing her address, he could not divorce her, he thought. He still had feelings for her and thought about her often. His rage of how she had disappeared had left him. He was satisfied he had convinced most people that it had all been Emily's fault for the breakup.

Margaret and Brian invited Neil for Christmas dinner, like the old days. He brought them gifts as he had done before. An electric drill for Brian and an electric food mixer for Margaret.

They both thought the world of Neil – to them, he was their son. It was Emily they were angry at, for leaving poor Neil alone. If they ever found her, they would drag her back to Neil.

Emily and Ken were not seen again, no one had any idea what had happened to them. No one had seen them both, sat chatting in Ken's new van in Townsfoot that day, the day she disappeared.

LIFE CONTINUES

Neil continued to concentrate on building the new cowshed. He wanted to expand his business.

His evenings were spent mostly at meetings and the pub. He began chatting more and more with Janet; people were whispering about it behind his back.

"Neil can't marry her until Emily is found or Emily divorces him," laughed a neighbouring farmer.

"You're right there, Ben. It won't stop him bedding her, though," another voice chipped in.

"What if he gets her pregnant, then what?" the farmer asked.

"It'll be illegitimate, it won't have the same rights to the farm," said a younger voice.

Neil waited another year before he asked Janet out on a date. Janet was very keen on him and accepted. He took her to the grandest hotel for a meal, about twenty miles away, so no one would know.

Janet knew the circumstances and knew they couldn't get married, but she loved the attention and the expensive meals.

Neil started giving her expensive gifts of jewellery. He hadn't sold Emily's jewellery as he had told her parents – Janet was being gifted with them! They even went on secret holidays together.

Janet was falling more and more in love with him and wished she could move in with him. Neil was playing things safe. He didn't want Emily turning up and destroying his net worth by divorcing him!

In 1977 Neil couldn't wait anymore for his wife to show up or divorce him. He was utterly fed up with the situation Emily had put him in. He was full of hate for her for taking away his control over his life. Neil decided to ask Janet to move into Meadows Farm with him.

He hadn't seen a solicitor; he didn't use them. So, he hadn't found out he could have divorced Emily after 5 years; providing he had diligently made an effort to find her. He was expecting Emily to divorce him and marry Ken.

Neil and Janet continued being on the same committees, going to the meetings and to the pub afterwards. It had caused quite a scandal, Janet moving into the farmhouse. There was a lot of gossip amongst the locals.

Neil was over the moon when Janet became pregnant. He showered her with gifts and couldn't love her enough.

When their son was born in 1978, Neil was an exceptionally proud father. It was something Emily had never managed to give him. He still hated her as he could still not marry Janet, so he thought.

Neil still saw Brian and Margaret at Browtop farm. They still treated him like a son. They didn't blame him for taking another woman. They thought Emily should have had the decency to have divorced Neil by now.

Janet gave birth to a baby girl, called Jenny in 1980. Neil was very happy, he had a complete family now, but he did desperately want to marry Janet.

It was 1st November 1982 when their lives were shattered with the discovery by the police. The female skull and male leg bone had been found in the wood.

Neil received a telephone call on the Tuesday evening while he ate his supper. The strange voice informed him, "Janet answered the phone when I rang before. I thought you would be crawling with police and I said I would ring later."

"Who are you and what do you want?" Neil asked. He was very annoyed at his supper being interrupted.

The strange voice continued, "You don't know me, but I saw you bury your wife, Emily, in the wood that night. I was walking on the road and saw lights, so I walked down to watch you." There was a pause.

"I want £5,000 to keep my mouth shut," said the strange voice.

Neil was explosively angry.

"Go to hell, you sick bastard." Neil slammed down the phone in anger.

Janet heard him shouting and asked what had upset him. Neil just told her it was some weirdo and left it at that.

26th November 1971 was the day Emily had disappeared. She was sat chatting to Ken in his blue Commer van. She cried when she mentioned Jet had been killed. Ken tried to comfort her.

Later Ken asked her if she wanted to share his flask of tea and cake, and they continued to chat. She thought what a lovely kind man he was.

Ken got out a wad of cotton wool and placed it on his knee. He poured some liquid onto it from a small bottle while still chatting away.

"What are you doing?" asked Emily naively.

"I've got sinus problems – this helps to relieve it," Ken replied convincingly.

"It smells awful," Emily said, beginning to cough. Suddenly Ken put the wad of cotton wool over her nose. She fought desperately to remove it.

The breath from her body was quickly disappearing with the ether being breathed into her lungs.

She fell into unconsciousness. Ken wound down his window to get rid of the smell of ether. He drove her to his newly rented cottage on the isolated boundary of a farm estate in Farnton.

Whenever he thought she was coming around; he gave her another dose, to make sure she would remain asleep until he had her safely in the cottage.

He carried her into the cottage over his shoulder. He walked down the stairs to the cellar. He removed her coat and left her there. He locked the door behind him. He was so pleased he had got her. She is mine now, he thought.

He carried a mattress and bedding into the cellar and laid her on it. Emily was beginning to come around.

"Where am I?" Emily moaned.

"You're here with me, my darling, I'll take care of you, I'll not hurt you ever. You're safe with me." Ken soothingly stroked her hair.

"What are you doing, where am I?" Emily said, struggling to get up.

Ken gently held her down. He smiled at her.

"You're at my newly rented cottage, just relax, my dear, I'm going to make us some tea." Ken left the room.

Emily was slowly realising what was happening. She became aware of her right ankle; it felt heavy. She looked at it and became very frightened.

Ken had put a padlocked chain around her ankle, the long length of chain extended to the wall. There it was padlocked to a ring on the wall.

She quickly looked around the room. She realised she was trapped in a cellar. The room was bare apart from some cardboard boxes, the mattress, bedding and a bucket.

There was a light bulb shining above; it was hanging from a cord from the ceiling. She could see a vent near the ceiling, probably at ground level, she thought.

The walls had been rendered but not painted, so the room looked drab and miserable, even with the light on. This was her prison, she thought. She hoped she would wake up from this terrible nightmare, but it was for real.

Ken came in with some mugs of tea and biscuits. She couldn't eat or drink – she felt sickened by what was going on.

"You must eat, my darling, to keep your strength up," Ken said very concerned. Emily turned away and cried.

Emily shouted through her tears, "You have no right to keep me here. I'm married, I belong with my husband, on Meadows Farm."

Ken's voice was kind when he replied to her. "I hope in time you will learn to love me, I will always love you, to the day I die; you are so beautiful. Neil didn't deserve you."

Emily sobbed. She thought her life had come to an end. Ken left her; he seemed genuinely upset. She could hear him walking around upstairs.

It was a very cold night. Emily had not got enough blankets to keep warm. She shivered in the dark. She just wanted to die; she had suffered so much these last few months.

Ken arrived the following morning. He was surprised and concerned at how cold Emily was and rushed upstairs for some more quilts and blankets.

She was grateful for the extra warmth and the hot tea and toast he brought in. Ken was not going to work that day; it was a Saturday.

He told her he was going to run a cable through the door frame, to provide her with electricity. She could then have an electric fire to keep her warm in the cold winter months.

He made her some hot soup in a mug with a bread roll for lunch. He ate with her too, to keep her company. She began to relax with him a little. She was being fed and kept warm, she thought – she may yet survive this ordeal.

He was obviously out of his mind to do this to her, but in his own thoughts he was doing the right thing. She thought if she was nice to him, he would eventually let her go.

On the Sunday, Ken brought down a proper bed into the cellar and a table with two chairs. He brought her some reading books.

Later he reassembled a small wardrobe in the cellar for her. She was glad the room was looking better to live in.

Ken constructed a commode out of a wooden chair and brought down a bowl of warm water for her to wash herself in. She felt better for freshening up. She combed her hair with a comb he had given her.

The next day, he had made her porridge, bacon and eggs and a mug of tea, for her breakfast. He laid it out on the table for her.

"I'll have to go to work today, but I'll be back about 5.30 pm," he softly told her. "I'll bring you some underwear and other clothes for you. Here are some sandwiches and water for lunch." He passed them to her, smiling lovingly at her.

Later Emily could hear the van drive away. She desperately tried to ease the chain down her ankle and foot, but it was no use. Her chain was long enough to allow her to lift one of the chairs to the wall with the vent.

She could easily see the outside. The fresh breeze on her face reminded her of the farm. She felt so homesick for both of the farms and the animals.

She could only see the sky, a path and a garden wall. The sky was grey and threatening – it's going to rain soon, she thought. She began to scream and yell at the top of her voice but there was not a sound from outside.

She got into bed and sobbed. She wished Jet was there to comfort her. She hoped the police were out looking for her. Neil would have reported her missing by now. She had to survive; they would find her eventually – it was her only hope.

The hours crawled by. She tried to think about the routine at home – time seemed to zip by there. She thought she should start organising a routine to make the time go quicker and keep herself sane. Meals, exercise, and reading.

Shouting through the vent, say, on the hour every hour, then she would remember. There could be someone passing by, she hoped, or a postman. Her wristwatch would keep her on track.

The wind blew straight through the vent as a storm raged outside. She tore off some cardboard from a box and covered the vent, wedging some into the slits to secure it.

Her mood sunk into depression. She could only think of gloomy thoughts. She lay in bed, her routine already forgotten.

Ken arrived with tea. Emily always used to call it supper. It was cottage pie and vegetables and cake to follow. It was bought from a shop, he told her, Mrs Dunlop the shopkeeper had made the cottage pie for him but he was given the cake from a customer on his rounds.

They both sat at the table and ate, although Emily wasn't hungry and left half of hers.

"Perhaps I'm feeding you too well?" Ken said kindly.

He brought in a box to show her the contents.

"Here are some clothes and undies. It was a bit embarrassing buying ladies' things, particularly the feminine hygiene products."

He lifted each item out of the box for her to inspect them. He was very pleased with himself at looking after her so well.

"Here is a toothbrush, toothpaste and soap. Now have I forgotten anything?" he said excitedly. Emily didn't reply – she felt too miserable.

Later she was thinking what she could do down there to pass the time away.

"It was very boring today; I have nothing to do all day. Can I have a bat and ball? It will keep me exercised," Emily asked, almost in tears.

"Of course, you can, I want you to be happy while I'm away." He smiled tenderly at her.

"Is there anything else?"

"I miss the animals and the farm – please let me go back home." Emily burst into tears; she desperately wanted to leave.

"There, there now. Don't upset yourself. I know, I'll bring you a lovely surprise tomorrow. That will cheer you up, my darling."

He brought down the radio for her to listen to and offered to read to her. She was thankful he didn't leave her alone all the time or she would have gone mad.

The following day she was feeling down – the day seemed longer than the day before. She spent a lot of time crying, curled up in bed, her radio blaring out music.

Ken arrived with the tea. Fish pie and vegetables, followed by ice cream. He was very cheerful and chatty as he sat down to dine with her.

"Oh yes," Ken said laughing. "I've forgotten the bat and ball; they are in the kitchen." He dashed to get them for her.

Later he said, "I have a lovely surprise for you, it's in the van. I'll get it for you." He ran off excitedly to fetch it. Emily wasn't really bothered and went to sit on the bed playing with her bat and ball.

"Meow, meow" she heard. Her eyes opened wide and she smiled. It was a black and white kitten.

"Oh, thank you," she cried and took the kitten from him and cuddled it. She called the kitten Whiskers.

"It will want some food and milk," Emily said, choking on her words with emotion.

"I've thought of that." He ran to fetch them. "Here is some fish and a little milk." He passed her a small bowl of mixed fish and a bowl of milk.

He was so happy that she had smiled at last. He was pleased she liked her surprise. He thought of other surprises he could get her to make her happy.

The following day was bearable, she had a companion. She made a ball out of some cardboard. She smiled at it running around trying to catch the ball.

She remembered on the hour every hour to scream and yell out of the vent then return the cardboard cover to stop the draughts. Sadly no one heard her.

She trained the kitten to use the bottom of the cardboard box she had ripped off, as a toilet.

The room after a while began to stink, with the smell from the commode and the kitten's toilet. She had to open the vent for some fresh air. There was about an inch gap under the door to create a draught through the room.

Ken arrived with tea and laid the boiled eggs and buttered bread on plates at the table. He had brought a trifle to follow.

Emily told him about the smell and suggested making compost toilets using soil to eliminate the smell. Her urine could be collected in bottles. He thought that was a good idea.

He saw that Emily's ankle was sore and bleeding from the chain, cutting into her skin. He tenderly bathed it and bandaged around the wound to make it more comfortable.

How could he be so loving and caring on the one hand and keep her prisoner on the other? Emily thought as he finished the dressing.

"I'll go and wash up and then I'll read to you," Ken suggested removing the plates, dishes and cutlery.

"I've got these board games, Draughts, and Snakes and Ladders if you are interested. There are probably some playing cards somewhere, but I've not finished unpacking from the move." Ken had remembered as he walked through the door.

Emily thought she may as well play the board games – at least it was better than being on her own. It would also pass the time.

This had become the routine; some days she was brighter than others. At least he had not tried to touch her and was being kind, in a way. He was just probably very lonely and wanted company, she thought, trying to make sense of the bizarre situation she was in.

In her very depressed moments, she would think of the animals that she had dearly loved. Jet, Melody, Ben, Nipper, Molly, Spot, Lotty, the blind calf, and all the cats and kittens.

She would visualise them in her mind one at a time. She tried to remember every adorable moment she had shared with them. It brightened her up and brought her out of her gloom.

The Christmas holidays had arrived. There was snow on the ground, she could see it though the vent. Ken had made a metal cover for the vent; one she could remove for fresh air.

The kitten had grown and was very playful. It was a delight to brighten her darkest days. Ken had a week off around Christmas.

He spent most of the time with her. Joining her playing with the ball. They even chalked on the floor and played hopscotch together. Emily, holding up her chain. She even laughed once at their childish play.

On Christmas Day he brought in a black Labrador puppy. Emily cried as she cuddled the cute little thing. It reminded her of Jet.

"I'll call her Mel," Emily announced. She would have to toilet train her, so a large metal box was brought in and filled with soil.

"I'm going to take your chain off," Ken said softly. Emily smiled – she hated the chain.

"Now don't run away or I'll kill your pets," Ken said sternly. She worried; he would eventually kill her in the end.

Emily almost felt, a little happiness, she had her pets, she was well fed and every night she had Ken's company. She was even smiling again and occasionally laughed at the antics of her animals.

She spent hours training her puppy to walk to heel, sit when told and to come when called. Even her kitten tried to copy as well. Both of the pets adored each other and would play and sleep together.

Emily continued her routine of screaming and yelling on the hour marked by her watch. At times the enthusiasm just wasn't there. If only someone would hear her, she wished.

She actually started looking forward to Ken coming home. It broke up the monotony of being so alone in her prison.

Ken was having to do all the work, emptying three compost toilets and bringing in fresh soil; making or fetching meals, washing up and washing clothes and linen; bringing in warm water for her to wash in and disposing of it.

Emily was still not allowed out of the room. She had tried to escape through the door but it was a heavy door with a big lock on it. She knew she had another locked door at the top of the stairs to negotiate with, even if she could unlock the first one.

She realised if she did escape, she would not have a coat to wear. Ken had taken that from her. She would freeze to death in these temperatures outside. She didn't know how far she would have to walk to the nearest house. She had no idea where she was living.

For her birthday, Ken had bought her a birthday cake complete with twenty-one candles. When she blew the candles out, she wondered how long she would have to survive in captivity.

He showered her with gifts: a sewing machine, a sewing basket, knitting needles, wool and material. She felt very lucky.

At least she had not been captured by a sadistic killer and was being tortured every day. She was living quite well, compared to that, she thought.

In the spring Ken announced they were moving. Emily wondered if it was her time to escape. While she had turned away from him the following day, he slipped, out of a bag in his pocket, a wad of cotton wool soaked in ether.

Emily swung round; she would never forget that smell. Ken was too quick – he had it over her nose before she could defend herself.

Ken bungled her into the back of his van. Mel and Whiskers were put in the front in a box. He drove to another isolated cottage and unloaded them all.

When Emily came too, Mel was licking her face. Ken was nowhere in sight. She struggled to the door to escape, but it was locked.

She looked around the room – it was a bedroom. Light streamed through slits in the closed shutters outside.

There was a proper bed, cupboards, wardrobe and drawers, and even a carpet on the floor. There were curtains at the window and a shade on the light hanging from the ceiling.

She opened a door and it led into a bathroom with a three-piece bathroom suite. Both Whiskers and Mel followed her in, to look. She was amazed – this was luxury compared to what she was used to.

Ken arrived. He had gone back to collect the rest of their belongings.

"It will be a lot better for you," Ken said, smiling. "You'll be able to train your pets to go into the bathroom to their toilets."

Emily smiled – it was so ludicrous: he loved her so much he wanted her to be comfortable but still a prisoner; at least she had some luxury now.

He gave her a red collar and lead for Mel and a white collar for Whiskers. He was pleased it made her smile, he wanted her to be happy.

The following day he brought in a television! The table and chairs they had at the other place were brought in for their meals.

Emily's routine after breakfast when Ken had left for work was established. She would wash. She would do her exercises, bending, stretching and lifting. Sometimes she would then have a long lazy bath.

She spent time training her puppy and kitten in toilet training, no more compost toilets, everything could be poured into the toilet and flushed away. The small window in there was frosted glass and appeared to be impossible to open.

She would construct an assault course out of the furniture for her and the puppy to climb, jump and crawl under. Sometimes Whiskers would join in. After, she would spend time grooming both of them with brushes Ken had given her.

Then she would relax and read a book with the music from the radio in the background. She had never really liked reading but now she found it very interesting. It was mostly fiction novels and some of the classics like Jane Eyre by Charlotte Bronte.

She would eat her sandwiches and drink the water left by Ken for her dinner at about 12 noon and watch the BBC News on the television. She hoped to hear any news about the search for her. But nothing was ever mentioned.

In the afternoon she would knit or sew, listening to the radio. Mel and Whiskers would play together after their nap. She would pause to watch them play; thankful they were with her.

The days started to fly by. Ken had given her a sketch pad. She practised drawing Mel and Whiskers while they were asleep, before she started her sewing.

She always had plenty to do, if she could keep her motivation going. There were days that she lost hope; she didn't do the screaming and yelling on the hour every hour here. There was no point – she couldn't get the windows open.

She had seen the farmer on the tractor checking the fences. She had banged on the window, and screamed and yelled, but he couldn't hear her. Her heart sank when he turned the tractor to leave the field.

Ken didn't arrive home for tea one night. She was very worried; she depended on him for everything. What if he had been killed in an accident? No one would know she was here. She would have to break out somehow.

She could smash the glass in the window with a chair, she thought. Could she smash the shutters and lower Mel and Whiskers to the ground below in a sheet, without them jumping out to their deaths?

Around 7 pm Ken's van could be heard parking outside. Emily was relieved.

"Sorry I'm late, darling. I had a flat tyre coming home and had to deal with that. I've bought some fish and chips for us."

THE BEGINNING OF THE END

Emily had sussed out that the top floor she was on had only the one room. Ken must be sleeping downstairs in the sitting room.

She could hear a key being turned in another door from hers. It was opened then shut and the key turned again, then she would hear Ken climb the stairs and turn the key in the lock of her door. So, she still had two locks to negotiate if she escaped using that route.

She thought he must be washing himself at the kitchen sink as he never used the bath upstairs. Strange, she thought, he has given her the luxury and deprived himself!

There must be an outside toilet as he didn't use the one in the bathroom. Perhaps it was originally a two-bedroom cottage with an outside toilet. Then the smaller bedroom was converted to an en-suite bathroom.

It was probably a farm worker's cottage on the boundary of a farm somewhere, she pondered. She wondered why the postman never came to this cottage or the last one.

Perhaps Ken made arrangements to collect his post from the Post Office, so she could not alert the postman in any way, she reasoned.

Emily tried to open the bedroom window again, but it was impossible. Through the slits on the shutters she could only see fields, no roads. There was a wooded area to the left.

If only she could get the window to open, she could perhaps wave a sheet through the slits of the shutters and attract the attention of the farmer when he was driving his tractor through the field again, she wished.

It was no use: Ken must have secured the windows from the outside and the shutters too. Would she ever escape or be found? she wondered.

This move was not the only move she would have; they moved around quite often. She lost track of how many times – it could have been about ten. Sometimes she was imprisoned in basements; other times in the upper rooms. Never on the ground floor.

She assumed the frequent moves were to do with Ken's job. Likely he had to find new areas to sell his wares, to new people.

Ken would blindfold her, going to the van. He would threaten to kill Mel and Whiskers if she made any attempt to escape. He would hold Mel on a lead and Emily would carry Whiskers. Then he would bundle them all in the back of the van.

They arrived at a new location. Emily had no idea where in the country she was. She was locked in the two upper rooms. There was a bedroom and a separate bathroom. It was very cold when she moved in. It was the end of October 1982. Ken got the central heating working and the electric fire going, to heat the place up.

After everything was unpacked, her usual routine began. She had checked if she could open the two windows. Ken must have secured them again from the outside.

Shutters blocked her view; there was only a small diamond shaped hole in the middle of each shutter. She knew she was in a remote location again when she saw the woods and fields through the holes.

There were no roads, so she assumed she was at the back of the house again. She had her television and radio and more or less the same furniture in her room.

She had learnt to crochet and paint in water colours, something she had never tried before. She would paint the scenes she remembered of Browtop and Meadows Farm. The time would go very quickly with all her craft work, reading and exercising her pets and herself.

In the evenings and holidays, Ken would spend his time with her. He was still kind to her and got her anything she asked for – apart from her freedom. She was still afraid he would eventually kill her in the end.

She did plead with him to let her go home but he would just say, "I know, I'll bring you a surprise home to cheer you up, my darling."

He never once tried to kiss her. It seemed that her company was enough for him and he wanted to support her and take care of her. He never shouted at her or hit her.

They had been there a few days when Emily's ears pricked up. Meadows Farm in Finley near Townsfoot was mentioned on the television! She stopped eating her sandwiches and listened intently. Her jaw dropped in a surprised way.

The broadcaster was reporting about a young female skull and a young male leg bone. They had been found in the wood after a flash flood had exposed them.

The farmer, Neil Dale, and his partner, Janet Bennett, had both been questioned. No arrests had been made. It was a double shock to Emily. She couldn't believe he had forgotten about her and got another woman.

Had Neil anything to do with the bones? Had he murdered them in one of his rages? She had so many questions whirling around her head.

That afternoon she couldn't concentrate on her sewing or knitting. If she did get away from Ken what was there for her in the outside world? She would hate to go back and live with her parents.

Were her parents still doting on Neil, or had they stopped after being so disgusted he had taken on a partner?

Emily didn't know whether to tell Ken. She decided not to; it would be her secret. She would still have to keep her rings on; or else Ken would know she had found out about Neil's partner.

Ken came home at the usual time 5.30 pm. He had brought home tuna fish pie and vegetables and lemon meringue pie.

He was very cheerful and chatty as usual. Emily didn't feel hungry. She managed to keep the television off by asking to play Monopoly and chess, that he had taught her to play.

Ken saw the article about the double murder at Meadows Farm, in the newspaper the following day. He read that Emily's husband, had another partner and decided not to upset Emily with the bad news.

Ken walked into the Post Office and store in the village on his way home as he usually did.

"Hello Mr Walker, and how are you today?" asked the lady behind the counter.

"I'm very well, thank you, is there any post for me today?" Ken inquired.

"I'll have a look... only one today, here it is," she said cheerily. "We could deliver your mail if you wish – a van goes in that direction every day, apart from Sundays," the lady informed him.

"No that's quite alright, I pass here every day to go home from work," Ken replied, smiling.

"What do you do for a living, Mr Walker, if you don't mind me asking?"

Ken was pleased to tell her. "I'm a salesman and very successful as well. I've built up a business from small household items to larger electrical goods like portable sewing machines, hair dryers and toasters."

"I would be interested to take a look on my day off, I could do with another toaster," she said, laughing.

"How is Mrs Walker these days?"

Ken had forgotten he had told her he had an invalid wife, when he had to buy some tampons, in an emergency.

"She is as well as can be expected. She will be enjoying this lovely sunshine through the window, today, I expect," Ken told her, lying as convincingly as he could.

Ken left as the lady's brother entered the shop.

"How are you, Kate?" her brother Jim asked.

Kate was sorting out some papers and looked up at him.

"Do you know that man who has just left the shop?" Kate asked him.

"No, should I?" Jim replied, getting his wallet out.

"I think he is strange somehow. He's polite and friendly and all that, but why doesn't he have his post delivered like everyone else?" Kate asked him.

"You're more suspicious than me and I'm a copper!" he replied.

"He only gets post, never his wife," Kate continued. "Why do we never see her? Poor soul, she is an invalid, he told me and they live so isolated. She should be getting some kind of benefit in her own name by post, shouldn't she?"

"Perhaps he deals with everything in his name. If she is in a wheelchair it is probably very difficult to get her about," Jim assumed.

"I could give you his name and address. You could at least check-up to see if he is married," Kate enthusiastically told him.

"And what should I tell my boss if he asks? ... using police resources on a suspicion my sister has!" Jim laughed rather amused.

"I thought that was what the police were there for, to check out suspicious characters," Kate argued.

"He hasn't done anything suspicious in the eyes of the law, Kate, so drop it," Jim said abruptly.

Kate was determined to get to the bottom of it; her intuition knew something wasn't right. The next time Ken came in to the shop, she smiled warmly at him.

"Hello Mr Walker, lovely day again, your wife will be enjoying seeing the sunshine out of the window again... We are having our annual indoor village fete next week. Would you both like to come? I'm sure your wife would like to get out and meet us all. Here is a leaflet about it all."

"I'll ask her, see what she would like to do," Ken said, a little annoyed at being pressured.

"Sorry, no post today for you or Mrs Walker." Kate smiled. "Is there anything else, Mr Walker?"

"Have you got any of those homemade pies you do?" asked Ken. Kate wrapped a couple up in a brown paper bag for him and Ken paid and left.

Kate didn't see the Walkers at the fete. Every time she saw her brother, she would pressurise him to at least check they were married.

Jim was starting to take note of the odd behaviour. He did check and found out he wasn't married. His name on his driving licence was Alan Walker, the same name on his letters.

"They could be living in sin," Jim explained to his sister. Kate was even more suspicious now.

Jim thought he would take a drive over to the cottage to see if he could talk to this mysterious wife and settle the matter.

Emily heard a car drive up and park at the front of the house. It was in the middle of the day. She hoped it wasn't a burglar.

There were a few loud knocks at the door. Burglars don't knock, she thought. She began screaming and yelling, Mel started barking. Unfortunately, Jim didn't hear them as he walked round the side of the cottage, to the back.

He saw the shutters had been barred up. He began to shout, "Police, is anyone there?"

Emily screamed as loud as she could and threw a chair at the window; the glass shattered into pieces. She banged on the wooden shutter but it wouldn't open. She continued to scream and yell. Mel ran around barking frantically. Whiskers looked startled.

"I hear you; I will try to get in," Jim shouted.

Jim called for backup. He smashed a lower window and climbed in.

"Are you alright?" he shouted, trying to open the door to the stairs.

"Please help me," she cried.

"I'm trying to find the key, hold on," Jim called out, searching the cupboards. He found some keys hanging up inside a top cupboard.

He tried each one in the lock; it opened. He ran upstairs and tried the next key. Emily's heart was pounding – she never thought this day would come.

Jim burst into the room. Emily was overjoyed and ran and gave him a big hug.

"Thank you, thank you," she cried, tears streaming down her pale face. Jim hugged her and looked around the room.

Mel was excitedly racing around barking, Whiskers was purring and brushing against Jim's legs.

"Are you alright? What is your name?" Jim asked her, gently pulling her away from the hug.

Emily could hardly speak she was so emotional and choked up. She just cried.

"Don't worry, you are safe now," Jim said, drawing her into another hug.

When Emily managed to compose herself, she told him her name: Emily Dale, Mrs Dale from Meadows Farm in Finley near Townsfoot.

Jim had never heard of it, but he contacted base and relayed the information through. More police arrived.

Emily told them that Ken had kidnapped her on 26th November 1971. Eleven years ago.

They told her his real name was Alan Walker. Emily was very shocked. She told them they had lived in many places but didn't know where.

"Please don't take my pets away; they are my only friends," Emily pleaded. She had seen one of the policemen was putting a lead on Mel.

"Don't worry, we are going to take them to the car with you and take you all to safety, to the police station," the policeman said kindly.

Emily was questioned by Jim there, with a policewoman present. He wanted to know everything about her kidnapping and captivity. They were in a family room with sofas and a carpet. In the corner was a play box full of toys.

She was offered tea and biscuits and everyone was very kind and understanding towards her.

Jim was exceptionally kind with her and seemed to know what she had been through. There was a box of tissues on the table and Emily was constantly dipping in for a tissue. It was painful and emotional telling her story.

She shook with nerves – she hadn't spoken to another human being for eleven years, apart from Ken. There was such a lot to take in, it was all very overwhelming for her.

Mel and Whiskers were allowed to stay with her, as she was distraught if they went out of her sight. They had never been parted before. They had been prisoners as much as she had been and were fretful.

"Would you like your parents to be informed of your whereabouts?" Jim asked quietly.

"I don't even know where I am!" Emily cried, totally confused. Jim told her they were in Devon at the main police headquarters in Riddleton.

Jim had been informed that Emily was from Yorkshire and that her husband had taken in a new partner.

"Yes please, ring my parents, I still remember their telephone number."

"We have been in touch with the local police there, we have all their details and your husband's details," Jim informed her calmly.

"I know Neil has another woman; I saw it on the television. He won't want me now." Emily sobbed. "Where will I go now? I have no money and no job."

"We will sort something out for you and your pets. In the meantime, you need to have a medical examination by a doctor, to see that you are fit and well after your horrendous ordeal."

All the police in the Devon area were on the lookout for Ken, now known as Alan Walker. He had changed his blue Commer van for a white Chevrolet van.

Police were at his home searching it and taking photographs for evidence. Eventually Alan was seen driving out of a farm road end.

He was pulled over and arrested for kidnapping Emily and holding her in captivity. Alan knew the game was up as soon as he saw the police car. He didn't resist the arrest and went into the police car quietly.

He immediately asked if Emily was alright and was informed that she was safe with her pets. Alan was relieved.

At the police station, he was interviewed in a small room without any windows. There was just a table and three chairs. He didn't want a solicitor present.

He told them he loved Emily. He wanted her to be happy and had done everything in his power to give her everything she wanted. He hated Neil for making her so unhappy, so that was why he had to kidnap her.

He confessed to another crime. When he was about twenty years old, he had kidnapped another girl aged eighteen years old. He thought he could make her very happy too.

"I rented a small house with a basement in Townsfoot; I put her in there. She started complaining of headaches and then started vomiting after a few days," Alan told them; he was shaking with emotion.

He burst into tears when he said, "I found her dead the next day.

"I loved her, I truly loved her, all I wanted was to make her very happy."

"What was her name?" the detective asked.

Alan had his head in his hands; he was rocking backwards and forwards.

"Gemma Whitehead, she was a lovely girl, I adored her," Alan said, crying uncontrollably.

"What did you do with her body?" was the next question.

Alan continued rocking and crying. He was genuinely sorry for her death but not the kidnapping. He thought he had done the right thing, to do that, in his twisted mind.

"I waited till dark, I put her in my van and drove her to Meadows Farm in Finley, where Emily used to live." Alan paused for a moment before continuing.

"There is a wood quite near to a road, I thought it would be the perfect place to bury her. I couldn't bury her very deep because of all the tree roots in the way. I covered the site with fallen leaves."

"Are you aware that we have found human remains in that wood?" Alan was asked.

"Yes, I read it in the newspaper – the skull will be Gemma's."

"Do you know anything about the leg bone from a young male?" Alan was asked.

"No, that's got nothing to do with me." He took his head away from his hands and looked up at his interviewers.

"You have got to believe me, it wasn't me, honest."

The interview carried on for most of the day and into the night. He was questioned over and over again. He remained consistent with every detail.

Alan was later charged with a list of offences for both cases. He did say that the last eleven years were the happiest years of his life spent with dear Emily.

A local policeman arrived at Meadows Farm. He wanted to speak to Neil on his own. Neil took him into the lounge.

"I have come to inform you, Neil, that your wife, Emily, has been found. She had been kidnapped and falsely imprisoned by Alan Walker, nicknamed Ken, for about eleven years."

Neil had to sit down – he was very shocked. All this time he had hated her for running off with another man and now he learns it was under very different circumstances.

"Is she alright? What did he do to her?" Neil demanded to know.

The policeman told him, "Emily is well and was not physically harmed."

"Where is she now? I'll go to her," Neil said, getting up to go.

"She is in Devon at present. She is aware you have a partner living here and have two children. Her expressed wish was not to see you."

Neil knew then he had lost her – if only he had waited, he thought. He knew now he should have reported her missing. He should have trusted her but he didn't. Now he knew she would divorce him. He stood to lose a lot.

Emily had a tearful conversation with her parents on the telephone. Her most burning question, she asked as soon as she could.

"Why didn't you report me missing?"

"Neil told us you had run off with Ken; we are very sorry. We know now we should have reported you missing but at the time, we were respecting your wish to be with Ken," her mother replied tearfully.

"Why do you always believe in Neil and not your own daughter?" Emily sobbed. Her mother handed the phone to Emily's father and broke down.

"Look, I know you are angry with us at the moment. You have had it tough, lass. You are very welcome to come home, we will take care of you," Brian said, speaking quietly.

"Thanks, Dad, but I have a lot to think about regarding my future plans. At the moment I'm all mixed up and I do not know what I want to do." With that Emily hung up. She felt so betrayed by everyone she had loved.

She sobbed and sobbed. At least Ken had cared for her, she thought. Mel and Whiskers cuddled into to her, sensing her distress.

Jim, Kate and their parents said they would take Emily into their home with her pets for the night until the police could sort out something permanent.

Kate was so pleased to see Emily. They were a similar age. Jim was about two years older. Emily had found out that it had been Kate who had set the ball rolling to find her, so she was extremely grateful and gave her a big hug.

She was introduced to their parents who welcomed her with a hug. She felt happier and more secure with a family around her.

Necessary belongings were bought from the cottage, she had been imprisoned in. The police had finished there and taken what they needed.

The trays the pets had been trained to use in the bathroom were brought. They had never toileted outside. They would have to be retrained on a lot of things.

Mel and Whiskers were both about eleven years old, so they also had a lot of adjusting to do. Mel had never run in a field! Whiskers had never hunted a mouse. They had never played outside or even seen snow. They had led such restricted lives.

Jim encouraged Emily to think positive – it was a new start in her life. She tried but there were so many unknowns. The world was a far different place than in 1971.

She hadn't driven a car, cooked, baked, worked or even been shopping in eleven years; it all seemed very intimidating to her.

"You must think in little baby steps, not at things as a whole," Jim recommended. "I will help you if you will let me."

"Thank you, thank you, Jim, I don't think I can manage on my own," she cried, truly grateful for his help.

When Emily went to bed that night, she pulled off the cluster diamond engagement ring and the wedding ring. She took off the sterling silver locket and put them all in her bag. It was the end of Neil and her, she thought.

She was glad as she knew she had not been happy with him. She hated the abuse and his presents did not make up for the love she longed for.

Kate, Jim and their parents talked that night after Emily had gone to bed with her pets. They had watched the national news about her escape from captivity.

Kate desperately wanted to help Emily in her recovery – she seemed so alone now that her husband had taken another woman. Jim felt the same.

Secretly Jim had fallen in love with Emily when they had first met and hugged. He wanted her to be able to cope with life before entering into the big bad world again.

JUSTICE

Emily had learnt that Mr Cooper ran the Post Office and store with Kate. Her mother, Mrs Cooper, was a part-time nurse.

Kate was engaged to an electrician called David and they were soon to be married. Jim was a police detective. It was a large house the Coopers lived in, with three floors.

The ground floor was the Post Office and shop, with a store room, a small office and toilet at the back. On the first floor, there was a large kitchen, dining room and lounge. On the second floor there were four bedrooms and a bathroom.

Emily went downstairs with her animals the following morning; they were very clingy and would not let her out of their sight. This was a strange new world to them. She went into the light, airy kitchen.

"Can I help make breakfast?" she asked.

The radio was on and Mrs Cooper was making porridge.

"You don't need to, my dear."

"I need to earn my keep as I have no money to pay you for the board and lodgings," Emily said with tears in her eyes.

"Bless you, my dear, after all you have been through. You are our most welcome guest in this house and are not required to work."

Emily ran to give her a big hug. She felt so overwhelmed with the kindness of these wonderful strangers. One by one everyone arrived for breakfast.

The Post Office had been open since 6 am; the other three had been sorting newspapers for the newspaper rounds.

Jim asked Emily if she would like a walk out with Mel. She agreed as long as she could take Whiskers in a bag with her. She was afraid Whiskers might fret without her.

Mel was excited to smell every lamp post, smelling other dogs. She had not seen another dog since she was a pup.

The first dog Mel did meet, she didn't quite know what to do. She was wagging her tail but hid behind Emily's legs. Whiskers had poked her head out of the bag, wide eyed. She had never seen another dog before.

Emily was not used to this much traffic in her village and Mel was a bit afraid of the vehicles coming towards her and the noise. Once in the open field, she let Mel off the lead. Mel just looked and stayed close to her.

Jim chatted to Emily and asked her if she had any thoughts about returning home. She told him a little about her upbringing and didn't really want to go back to that again.

She had made up her mind to divorce Neil. She told Jim; her marriage hadn't been very happy.

"Will you help me get a solicitor to get the divorce moving straight away?" she asked.

"If you are sure that is what you want to do then I will make an appointment for you; you will have no problems getting a divorce."

Emily remembered she had no money! Jim said everything would be sorted out with the solicitor, she hadn't to worry.

That night Kate, David and Jim invited Emily to the local pub. She was a bit scared – she wasn't used to crowds, she thought it would be too overwhelming for her to cope with and declined.

They didn't press her; she had to do things in her own time, they thought. Emily started doing odd jobs in the house as part of her recovery process.

There was a phone call – Jim answered it. It was a national newspaper wanting an exclusive on Emily's story. They were offering her a large lump sum in advance. Jim said he would discuss it with her.

Jim told her it would help her set up a new life for herself, buying a home, car and everything else she required.

"I've nothing else so I may as well earn my keep with it." She sighed, not sure if it was the right thing to do.

An interview with a reporter was arranged. Emily insisted Jim had to be present. It was quite an ordeal going through everything again, she often choked up remembering the details. She was angry that eleven years of her freedom had been taken away from her.

Newspapers with the article were quickly sold out. Many people knew Ken, the salesman, or by other aliases and also by his real name Alan Walker. At least people that had known Emily in her home area would finally know the truth – she was happy about that.

Mrs Cooper let her do some baking another day. Emily had nearly forgotten all the recipes she had known. She accidentally dropped and smashed a dish, being so clumsy. She dropped to her knees and cried pitifully. She couldn't cope yet when things went wrong.

Mrs Cooper hugged her and kissed her on the forehead.

"It's only a dish, my dear, it's not the end of the world. It can be replaced. You will get the hang of things in time, your confidence and self-esteem will come flooding back, you'll see."

The following week she received a solicitor's letter. She thought it was to do with the divorce, but it was a complete surprise. Alan Walker, or Ken as she knew him, had gifted her his van, furniture and business stock plus £10,000!

He thought she didn't have any money of her own. He wanted to make sure she could afford lodgings and food. She didn't know whether to accept it.

Jim said, "It's your decision but there are no conditions attached. He owes you a lot more for taking away your freedom. Besides, it will probably help his conscience."

Emily insisted on paying full board and lodgings and to help around the house and the garden. The van and other things were sold apart from a toaster for Kate and a new iron for Mrs Cooper.

Slowly Emily's confidence grew, her self-esteem was slowly coming back. Even Mel seemed more able to cope with the outside world. She loved to run in the field with Whiskers and playing there.

Whiskers would even stay with Mrs Cooper without fretting for Emily. Whiskers loved to curl up on her knee and fall asleep very content. Mrs Cooper had grown very fond of her.

Emily plucked up the courage to visit the pub with Jim, Kate and David; she was very nervous. Some people had recognised her as being the 'kidnapped woman' and stared at her. She learnt to sit with her back to the bar, so she would go unnoticed.

Jim and Emily were spending more time together when he wasn't working. He was slowly giving her the confidence to drive again, along isolated roads. Her confidence grew day by day.

He would take her shopping, to get her used to the crowds and traffic. Mel was content to stay with Whiskers, knowing Emily would return.

Jim helped her with the divorce, taking her to appointments with her solicitor which she found very nerve-racking.

She was so grateful for this family's support – she could never have done everything on her own. Jim was a tower of strength to her. She looked on him as a big brother.

Jim was over six-foot, average build and handsome. He had black hair and brown eyes. She had caught glimpses of him looking at her now and then and wondered if he liked her as a sister.

She heard Alan Walker had been sentenced at the Crown Court for Kidnapping and false imprisonment of her. He had a list of other offences to do with his other case, Gemma Whitehead.

He had eventually admitted to another kidnapping. The poor girl, Annie Wright, had suffered asphyxial death by ether. She had been his second victim. He had buried her on the Yorkshire Moors. He had pleaded guilty to all the offences. Emily thought she had been very lucky to be alive.

He would spend a lot of time behind bars. Probably never seeing his freedom again. She pitied him, in a way. If he had gone about things very differently, he could have made a good husband for someone.

She thought maybe it was the controlling he enjoyed as much as the caring. It certainly wasn't normal behaviour. He was definitely very mixed up at the role he had in life.

The police could not establish if Gemma, his first victim, had died of carbon monoxide poisoning due to the faulty boiler in the basement.

Alan had shown negligence – he didn't seek medical attention when Gemma was ill, which led to her death.

It was still a mystery about the leg bone in the wood. The police were waiting for this new DNA Science coming on the scene to eventually revolutionise Forensic Science.

Eventually DNA would confirm that the pulp from the molar in the skull was that of Gemma Whitehead.

Jim took Emily and Mel on a walk, through the fields. It was a beautiful day in the early summer of 1983. They sat down and chatted. They had just about learnt each other's life stories by now. Apart from a few little details.

Jim noticed the scars on her right arm. "Has someone bitten you?" he asked, very alarmed.

"It was my Dad's sheepdog," she replied and explained what had happened to her, when she was a young child.

Jim thought she looked so beautiful; he gently touched her dark chestnut curls. She flushed slightly. He leaned over and gave her a lovely warm kiss on her lips.

She hadn't really thought of him in that way. He was the big brother she never had, the rock she leaned on for support.

She thought she would never have a man in her life or ever get married again. She couldn't think of plans farther than a week into the future; she had so much to cope with.

"I'm sorry, I maybe shouldn't have done that?" Jim said apologetically.

"I'm not ready to get involved yet, I still can't cope with everything. You and your family have been so very kind to me, I'm very grateful to you all, for everything you have done for me." Emily smiled with tears in her eyes.

Kate and David got married and went to live in a cottage a few doors up from the Post Office. Kate still worked in the Post Office and shop.

Kate was a real friend, like a sister to Emily. They went shopping together and she would go to Kate's house for tea, on her days off.

Emily felt she had a loving, warm, stable family around her. She occasionally wrote to her parents and received replies from her mother. She definitely didn't want to live with them.

The Decree Absolute for the divorce arrived in the post. She had finally divorced Neil. She heard later from her mother that he had married Janet.

Emily knew once they were married, he would show his narcissistic side if he had not already done so. Women were just like property to him to be controlled, used and abused.

She had received a lump sum in the settlement agreement. She wasn't ready to live on her own, so continued to lodge with the Coopers.

As things in her life started to be sorted, she felt settled and actually happy with life. She was looking at Jim in a different way.

She thought he had noticed her glimpsing his way now and then.

They took Mel in the car to the coast for the day. Emily slipped her hand into Jim's while walking on the beach. Mel was running along ahead of them. Jim squeezed her hand gently; he was pleased she had done that.

They sat down on the sand. The sun and scenery were beautiful, the waves gently rolled onto the beach. Mel sat beside them quietly. Jim kissed her again; this time Emily responded.

They wrapped their arms around each other. Jim gently kissed her neck. She could feel his warm breath on her skin. She felt at peace again with life.

She felt the love encasing her, she was so happy to have a man like Jim from a loving, stable home. They lay down together and lovingly caressed. It was a wonderful feeling to be wanted like this again, she thought, excited her life had turned around at last.

The next year she was very happy: Jim and Emily regularly went out together or with Kate and David. She was beginning to bloom again; her eyes had that sparkle back. Her skin had a tan, once more. She often laughed and giggled, much to the delight of Jim.

He could see her coming back to life and was very happy for her. He loved her so much. All four of them suggested they go on holiday together. That mischievous glint in Emily's eyes, told Jim she agreed before she even said anything.

They travelled to Wales, after Jim got his holidays arranged with his boss. They stayed on a mountain side in a Bed and Breakfast place. They had to drive part of the way over bare rock to get there.

They spent their time walking further up into the grassy mountain, taking their packed lunches. On other days, they toured around Wales looking at the farming and tourist sights.

Emily had not had a holiday for years. She really enjoyed herself, particularly the company she was in. She loved the outdoors and especially the freedom.

When they got home, Jim was very busy at work for a while, but Emily didn't mind – she had Kate and Mr and Mrs Cooper's company to enjoy.

While Emily and Jim walked back home one night, a stranger appeared very distressed. He screamed out at them, "Cooper, this is for my brother."

A single shot rang out from a gun he was holding. The gun jammed on his second shot. He then ran off.

Everything appeared to be in slow motion to her; Jim clutched his chest and dropped to the ground. Emily dropped to her knees, screaming.

"Jim, Jim," she shouted. She looked round for anyone to help. They were alone.

"Help, help, someone please help us," she screamed frantically.

Someone ran around the corner towards them. He had heard the gun shot.

"I'll phone for an ambulance," he shouted.

Police and the ambulance arrived quickly.

Emily was able to give the ambulance crew Jim's details. The police questioned her. She was able to give a description of the person who shot Jim. She was very distressed and just wanted to be at the hospital to see that Jim would survive.

The policeman who questioned her was a friend of Jim. He drove Emily to the hospital and contacted the Cooper family. Jim was in the operating theatre having emergency surgery.

Emily was so grateful when Jim's family arrived and told them what had happened. It was very stressful waiting for any news.

Finally, they were told Jim would pull through.

Tears ran down Emily's face, tears of joy. They all hugged each other. They were there by his bedside when he came out of the general anaesthetic.

"You're not getting rid of me that easily," Jim joked, smiling at everyone looking so concerned.

The next time Emily visited; he was sat up in bed with a large bandage around his chest.

Emily took his hand and kissed him on the forehead.

"I love you, Jim, I was so scared I would lose you."

Jim smiled and looked into Emily's brown eyes. He lovingly stroked her hand.

"Will you marry me, Emily?" Jim asked, smiling.

Emily was not expecting that. She was very emotional; tears ran down her cheek as she replied, "Yes, yes, I would love to be your wife. I love you so much."

Jim grinned. "I've loved you since the day we met and I'll always love you and care for you."

Emily was so overwhelmed with happiness. She knew she had found her true soulmate at long last.

Jim spent a long time recovering in the hospital and at home. Emily was there to care for him and their love grew stronger.

When he was well enough, they both went out to choose a ring. She chose a round diamond engagement ring, she was grinning and giggling, she was very excited. Jim laughed with her; he was so pleased she was happy.

The Cooper family were overjoyed to hear they had got engaged. Emily felt she was a real member of this exceptionally warm, loving family.

They visited Emily's parents, Brian and Margaret, at Browtop Farm in Yorkshire. Her parents were very pleased to see her. They showed her the modernisation the landlord had done to the farmhouse – a proper bathroom and a fitted kitchen.

Emily showed them her ring and told them they were going to be married soon. They were polite to Jim, but Emily knew they weren't impressed. To them, Jim was not a landowner or farmer, so he was a big come down from Neil, in their eyes.

Jim and Emily stayed the night in the Midlands, on their way back home. They curled up together in the king-sized bed. It was a lovely decorated room, with pictures on every wall.

Jim's warm lips touched hers. She melted into his arms. His warm hands slid gently over her warm body, caressing her so lovingly.

Deep waves of love rippled through her body; it was a more mature, stable kind of loving, she had never felt before. The crescendo of feelings was magnified with this intense love Jim was pouring out to her. She adored every moment of this perfect euphoria.

They rolled onto their sides, their eyes closed, in perfect bliss. Jim cuddled her and they drifted off into a peaceful sleep together.

Back at Jim's house, Emily announced she wanted to buy the smallholding a mile away. It had recently come up for sale.

They both went to view the quaint little place. It had a kitchen, lounge and dining room downstairs. Three small bedrooms and a bathroom upstairs. It was called Rose Cottage.

There was a stable and a small stone barn and about two acres of land. It was ideal, Emily thought. Jim liked it too; he was pleased it wasn't isolated, it was next door to other houses.

They decided they would pay for it together. Jim had been saving for years for a place of his own. Now he was going to be married and this was going to be their very own home together.

Emily was very happy when a deal was finally agreed with the vendors. She spent a lot of time there, sometimes with Jim and sometimes on her own, painting and decorating. Mel and Whiskers would sometimes come to familiarise themselves, to their new home.

Both Jim and Emily went to choose furniture and material for curtains and covers. It was more exciting than moving into a man's house with everything complete as she had done with Neil. It was a wonderful shared experience with Jim, which brought them closer.

Their wedding day arrived on Saturday 7th April 1984. They had booked at the Registry Office in Riddleton. Emily wore a long sleek wedding dress to show off her gorgeous figure.

She had her hair gathered from the front to the back, with her curls cascading down her back. She wore Kate's diamond tiara.

Kate had applied Emily's makeup for her. Emily looked stunningly beautiful. Kate was her Matron of Honour. She wore a beautiful long pink dress with a purple sash.

Everyone turned to look at these stunningly beautiful women walking into the Registry Office that day. Emily's eyes sparkled. She was amongst the most loving and caring people she had ever known.

Mel and Whiskers attended; both had a purple bow around their necks. They were very well behaved. Emily's parents couldn't come. Her father had broken his ankle in a recent bad fall.

Jim had one of his colleagues for a best man – he was the policeman who was with Emily after Jim was shot. The wedding was mainly a close-knit family affair with an informal reception at a local hotel.

Jim couldn't take his eyes off Emily – she looked so regal and mature. She was ready to start her new life with him. He was determined to make the rest of her life extremely happy.

They honeymooned in Jersey for two weeks, enjoying the touring and sightseeing. Jim heard that the man who had shot him had been sentenced for attempted murder and firearm offences. Jim had investigated the case of his brother who had murdered several gang members; he had been sentenced to life in prison.

At Rose Cottage they had received a wedding card from Jill. She was married with two children. She wrote in the card, 'I hope you will be both be very happy and experience married bliss'. Emily remembered her saying at the cafe many years ago, 'married bliss is every girl's dream'.

The newlyweds, settled into a loving, stable, married life. Jim was everything Neil wasn't. Jim spent his spare time with her, taking her out, going on walks together, they enjoyed each other's company and were the best of friends.

Mel and Whiskers, both lived to a grand old age; they had spent a lot of their time with them. They were both there when their twin girls arrived home from hospital.

It was a very happy, loving home and family. Mel and Whiskers adored the twins.

Emily took in pet lambs that farmers didn't want to bottle feed. She helped at lambing time on a neighbouring farm after the girls started school. They had a few hens, pet rabbits, two fell ponies, a dog and a cat.

Emily, Jim and the twins, saw Emily's parents a few times but Brian never got on with Jim, as he had done with Neil. Her parents died in 1999 within six months of each other.

Janet had left Neil in the year 2000. Their daughter Jenny had already left home. Luke stayed and farmed with his father. Nigel Brown who found the bones, became the head stockman. In 2017 the cold case of the leg bone was reopened.

Only Mitochondrial DNA could be extracted from the leg bone, which would show the maternal ancestry. It was placed on the database for a match. It needed a family member from the mother's line to be on the database. No match.

However, in 2019, there was a match: a woman under the influence of drugs, had been convicted of stabbing a pedestrian. She was related to Joe Stokes, the homeless man. She confirmed none of the family or his friends, had seen him for years.

It wasn't long before the police made the connection to Neil, Joe's employer. Neil was arrested on suspicion of murder. He had been the last person to be seen with Joe and they were both very drunk at the time.

The police needed a confession. Neil told them Joe had left and that was all he knew. He was held in a police cell over night after questioning.

Neil was seventy-eight years old, overweight and in poor health. He suffered a massive heart attack and died in the police cell.

Emily heard the news on the television. It wasn't a shock about Joe – she knew what Neil was capable of. It was probably a blessing in disguise that Ken had kidnapped her. She would have probably been killed by Neil eventually in one of his rages. Perhaps even buried in the wood and she would have never have met Jim.

She'd had thirty-five years of blissful marriage so far with Jim. They were enjoying retirement together. Their twin girls, Charlotte and Louise, were both in the nursing profession. Emily had found the peace, love, happiness and stability she had always wished for in life.